TEA AND KISSES

"Good morning, Sir Evan. You are looking much better." She put the tray on the table beside the gentleman.

"I am feeling much better, madam. You have no need to worry that I shall be imposing on you for much longer, I do assure you."

Sarah shook her head as she poured his tea. "Do not worry yourself about that, sir. The boys have greatly enjoyed your company."

He couldn't resist the question that leapt into his mind. "And you?"

Her gaze never left her busy hands, but in a soft voice she replied, "I—I have as well." She handed him a cup of tea. Blue and emerald gazes locked. The air almost seemed to shimmer with electricity and his gaze lingered on her lovely mouth. Suddenly he was overwhelmed with an urge to crush her in his arms and taste those sweet lips. . . .

Books by Lynn Collum

A GAME OF CHANCE

ELIZABETH AND THE MAJOR

THE SPY'S BRIDE

LADY MIRANDA'S MASQUERADE

THE CHRISTMAS CHARM

THE VALENTINE CHARM

THE WEDDING CHARM

MISS WHITING AND THE SEVEN WARDS

Published by Zebra Books

MISS WHITING AND THE SEVEN WARDS

Lynn Collum

ZEBRA BOOKS
Kensington Publishing Corp.
http://www.kensingtonbooks.com

ZEBRA BOOKS are published by

Kensington Publishing Corp.
850 Third Avenue
New York, NY 10022

All Kensington titles, imprints and distributed lines are available at special quantity discounts for bulk purchases for sales promotion, premiums, fund-raising, educational or institutional use.

Special book excerpts or customized printings can also be created to fit specific needs. For details, write or phone the office of the Kensington Special Sales Manager: Kensington Publishing Corp., 850 Third Avenue, New York, NY 10022. Attn. Special Sales Department. Phone: 1-800-221-2647.

First Printing: August 2002
10 9 8 7 6 5 4 3 2 1

Printed in the United States of America

To Brian, Kyle, and Whitney,
thanks for all your support.

Prologue

"Where can that cursed mongrel be?" Lady Rosamund Dennison pushed back the branches of a small sapling as she peered into the thicket, searching for the headmistress's fat pug. The dense spring growth of new green leaves among the ancient ivy, blue periwinkles, and honeysuckle made her task all the more difficult. With a sigh, she straightened, pushing back loose blond curls, which were a nuisance, but the headmistress insisted that young ladies not yet out could not wear their hair up.

Lady Rose, as her friends called her, turned to the others. "Who would have thought huge, old Angus would have chased after a hare?"

In the middle of the clearing lay an old blue blanket filched from the stables of Parson's Academy for the Young Ladies of Quality with a large picnic basket and Lady Rosamund's closest friends, Miss Sarah Whiting and Miss Ella Sanderson. They were all dressed in regulation drab gray gowns with white lace collars. The three young ladies held the unfortunate distinction of being the oldest girls at the academy, having all reached the venerable age of nineteen. Unlike most of the young ladies who were removed at the tender age of eighteen and taken to London to make their bow to Society, the Three

Fates, as they had named themselves, remained all but forgotten by their families, spinning away their lives like Clotho, with the idle pursuits that the academy required.

Sarah, her long black hair carelessly tied with a white ribbon, called from a position at the edge of the blanket, "Do stop worrying about Angus. Unless I miss my guess, he shall be waiting at the kitchen door for his supper at precisely five o'clock, if he does not return sooner. He would never miss a meal."

Miss Ella Sanderson, her auburn curls coaxed into a neat braid at her neck, lifted the lid of the basket. "Come and try the tarts I baked this morning. We have so little time left before Sarah must take the stagecoach to Shropshire, and we shall soon depart as well." There was a bit of trepidation in the girl's voice. For all three there would be no grand welcome for their return home.

Miss Parson's retirement had at last forced the girls' families to finally remove them from school. To the headmistress's letter of announcement of the academy's closing there had been a staid reply from the Marquess of Denham that a coach would be sent for Lady Rosamund. A rambling letter came from Ella's aunt about the inconvenience of the timing, but a post chaise would be sent on the proper day. And lastly, a terse missive from Sarah's stepmother announced that a maid would arrive with sufficient funds for the girl to take the stagecoach home.

Lady Rosamund, after one last searching glance over her shoulder, lifted her skirt and made her way through the deep grass of the sun-washed meadow. The air was warm and fragrant with the scent of spring flowers, and she couldn't resist stopping to pick cowslips and phlox along the way. By the time she approached the blanket she had a lovely bouquet for their party.

As she stooped to pluck one last daisy, a furry gray streak flashed from the bushes behind her and knocked her off her feet, sending the bouquet flying. She sat up and glared at Angus, who settled on the blanket, sniffing the basket of food. Peals of laughter echoed in the meadow as the girls on the blanket enjoyed the sight of their friend with flowers at all angles in her hair, on her dress, and surrounding her.

Ella shook her head. "You look like one of those woods fairies in the paintings at my aunt's house."

Lady Rosamund glared at the canine. "Useless creature." Then a smiled tipped her mouth as the dog tried to lick Sarah's face, before settling on the blanket like an invited guest.

Suppressing her mirth, Sarah stroked the dog's head. While panting for breath from his morning exercise, he looked up at her and his pink tongue slid to one side. "You are lucky, my furry friend, that Lady Rose likes you or she would be using those flowers to put on your gravestone."

"I may yet if he doesn't remove himself from the blanket," Lady Rosamund called while she retrieved flowers from her hair.

Ella reached into the basket and took out a white napkin, unwrapping the bundle to reveal a small bone. "Look what Cook sent for you, Angus." She waved the bone in the air for the dog to get its scent, then tossed it to a stretch of grass beyond the blanket. The pug dashed after the treat and set upon it with great relish.

"Why, that looks like a beef bone." Lady Rosamund frowned, as she peered at the large joint that disappeared into Angus's jowls. "Wherever did

Cook find that, for I declare we've not had beef at Parson's in years." She settled herself on the blanket, tucking her bouquet into the wicker handle of the basket.

Ella continued to pass out the contents of the basket as she explained, "The butcher has a *tendre* for Cook. He sends little titbits along for her and she, in turn, shares what's left with Angus."

"A *tendre!*" Lady Rose's hazel eyes twinkled with amusement. "That grizzled old man is having thoughts of romance! Why, he looks more like a villain from one of Mrs. Radcliffe's novels with that craggy face and those scarred hands, not some dashing suitor."

Sarah sampled a piece of cinnamon bread and chuckled. "You'd best not say that to Cook for she thinks him the best of men. He is her knight in shining armor straight out of her own fairy tale. They are to be wed once the school is closed."

Ella sighed. "Oh, that life were a fairy tale, and we were going home to grand adventures with charming princes on white horses."

The three grew quiet as each contemplated her future. Lady Rosamund would return to a father who scarcely knew she existed; Ella must go to an aunt who planned to employ her as a companion to her daughters; and Sarah to a stepmother who couldn't stand the sight of her.

At that moment a lovely butterfly fluttered into their circle and seemed to break the dark spell. With a resigned sigh, Sarah said, "Shall we eat and think no more sad thoughts on such a glorious day?"

They set about their picnic, determined to enjoy this last full day of worry-free bliss. There were small cucumber sandwiches, fresh fruit and cheese, as well as cinnamon bread, tarts, and lemonade. The one advantage the girls had gained at Miss Parson's was that they had learned to cook, because punishment for any infraction entailed having to work in the kitchens for a full day, which saved on servants' salaries. In truth, Lady Rosamund, Ella, and Sarah had enjoyed their time in the fragrant recesses of the academy kitchens far more than they did any of the time they spent with many of the stern teachers employed by the sour Miss Parson. The girls were very often deliberately tardy for morning prayers or late with an assignment to earn such punishment.

The young ladies finished their meal and lay in the shade on their blanket, sharing their dreams. Lady Rosamund plucked petals from a daisy, saying, "I should love to spend my time riding on the moors all day long and dancing the night away at the local assemblies." Then she sighed. "But likely I shall spend my evenings in my room with Nurse while my father and his hunting friends drink the night away in the dining room."

The other girls exchanged a look that said their dreams were far less exalted. Ella sighed. "I should be happy if my cousins were to treat me as a member of the family and not some poor relation to be pitied and used as an unpaid servant."

Sarah nodded in agreement. "There is nothing like being treated as a stranger by one's relations. I should desire to have a family of my own, for my stepmama certainly doesn't consider me such."

Lady Rosamund tossed the denuded stem aside. "I say we make a pact that if one of us by some miracle has a change in fortune, she will invite the others to join her."

Ella and Sarah agreed, knowing that they were not likely to have to face such a possibility. With a giggle, they joined hands and cried "Pact." Then they fell to discussing other matters.

The spring air was warm and the skies clear, which caused them to linger and chat. Yet all the while they were spinning their fantasies, each knew that on the morrow harsh reality would be quite different.

A sudden bark from Angus announced the arrival of Alice Crum, a frail girl with mouse brown hair. Her torturously crimped ringlets had gone limp and begun to sag in the afternoon warmth. "There you all are. Miss Parson is in high dudgeon. I am certain she shall ring a peal over you all when I tell her where I found you, for we are never to cross the creek and leave the grounds."

Sarah sat up. "And just what good will your prattling do, Alice? We shall be gone by tomorrow. It would be most unkind of you to carry such a tale."

Alice lifted her chin, turning her back on Sarah. "I came all this way to tell Lady Rosamund her brother has arrived early and is waiting to escort her to York, and for my trouble, I am ill-used."

Lady Rose jumped to her feet. "Thank you, Alice. You may tell Miss Parson we shall be there directly."

"I am not some servant to be carrying messages, no matter who your father may be." The girl turned her back and stomped up the trail to the academy.

"Such a vile girl. I tried to befriend her when she first arrived but she would have none of it," Ella said.

Folding the blanket, Sarah said, "Her father's brother is an earl, so she likes to remind everyone."

Ella frowned. "So what does that make her?"

"Just a nasty-tempered girl, nothing more," Lady Rose said as she lifted the basket in preparation to leave.

In a great hurry, the three set off at a brisk pace. Ten minutes later they arrived back at the front hall of the aging manor house turned academy to find Lady Rosamund's brother, Lord Wingate, pacing the worn black-and-white tiles. Slender and blond like his sister, with a penchant toward foppery, he was attracting a great deal of attention from the young ladies lingering in the open parlor beyond the front hall.

At the sight of his sister, his lordship lifted his quizzing glass and looked her up and down from her windblown golden curls to her grass-stained gray dress. "Gad, Rosie, I see you are still the sad romp Papa sent away to learn some manners. He ain't going to be well pleased if you still cannot conduct yourself like a proper lady."

An angry flush stained her cheeks, but Lady Rosamund held her tongue. She straightened her shoulders, her chin going higher. "A fond welcome to you, Robert. Pray forgive my appearance, but we have been having a picnic. I am packed and shall join you in a moment." With that she swept up the stairs with all the dignity of a queen.

Sarah and Ella followed behind. They exchanged whispered opinions of Lady Rose's brother on the stairs and came to the conclusion that while he might be handsome in looks, his manner was not at all pleasing. In a hurried rush, the marquess's daughter was helped into a blue traveling gown by her friends. It was a bit too small, for her shape had grown more womanly in the three years since she'd arrived. With tears and kisses the trio made their farewells in the privacy of their small room, then Sarah and Ella accompanied the nervous girl down to the carriage where her brother was impatiently waiting.

The two remaining friends watched the carriage until it exited the grounds and was out of sight. The closed window did not allow Lady Rosamund one final wave.

"Do you think she will be kindly treated?" Ella worried.

Sarah shrugged. "I cannot say, but I hope her father's heart has grown fonder in her absence."

"Perhaps the marquess will have arranged for her come-out, for that is surely what is to be expected. What else would there be for her to do?"

Sarah locked her arm with Ella's. "Then we shall pray that is Lady Rose's fate." With a backward glance at the manor over her shoulder she added, "I think we might want to avoid seeing Miss Parson, for I feel certain that Alice has told of our leaving the academy grounds."

Ella nodded. "Shall we visit the shrubberies? It will give us more privacy." The girls set out for the south lawn, where an ancient maze was still maintained, hoping to enjoy the last of their day.

Surprisingly, at supper that evening they received only a mild scold from the distracted headmistress. She had other more important students on her mind than two orphaned girls whose relatives didn't even care enough to come for them in person.

Bright and early the following morning, the hustle and bustle of arriving parents began. By noon, most of the school was empty. At one sharp a maid knocked on Sarah and Ella's door, where they'd retreated to avoid the chaos, to announce that a post chaise was downstairs for Miss Sanderson. With a heavy heart, Sarah carried a piece of her friend's luggage downstairs.

As the post boy strapped Ella's cases to the back,

Sarah hugged her friend. "Be sure and write. I must know how you manage with your aunt."

"And you too must write and tell me how things go with Lady Whitefield." Ella climbed into the hired chaise and was soon waving from the window as the battered vehicle disappeared through the academy gates.

Sarah had never felt more alone. The two people who had meant the most to her since her parents had died so many years ago were gone, perhaps never to be seen again. Worse, she faced the prospect of going to live with a woman who had sent her here six years earlier and paid extra not to have her come home on holidays. Sarah had had great hopes long ago when her father had written from his yearly visit to London to say she had a new mother. Even in the early days when Lucinda Whiting, nee Granville, first arrived, Sarah thought herself the luckiest of girls, to have such a beautiful creature as a stepmother. But the lady had proven to be nothing like Sarah's mother, her rare beauty masking a dark heart. Lady Whitefield took an instant dislike to her new stepdaughter.

Things only got worse after Sarah's father died when she was thirteen. He'd scarcely been put into the ground before Lucinda summoned her stepdaughter to announce Sarah was being sent to Miss Parson's, where she would remain until she learned how to conduct herself properly. For years Sarah had blamed herself, for she had been rather a hysterical child at her father's funeral, knowing that she was truly alone. Yet all her letters of apology had garnered no reply from Lady Whitefield, and soon Sarah had come to realize that no matter her conduct, her stepmother would still have sent her away to school.

With dragging footsteps she turned and went back up to her room to await her turn to embark on a journey into the unknown. Two days would drag by before a lad from the local posting inn arrived in the inn's gig to take Sarah and her baggage to The Black Swan, where a maid was waiting to accompany her on her trip. As the boy raced the inn's only decent horse down the driveway, Sarah looked over her shoulder at Miss Parson's Academy and wondered if she would ever find such contentment and happiness again.

One

Her pink muslin morning gown molded to her elegant figure, Lucinda, Dowager Lady Whitefield, swept into the drawing room of the Whitefield Manor's dower house to greet her latest suitor. At two-and-thirty she had lost none of the beauty that had captured Lord Whitefield's attention over eight years ago. Her golden blond curls, covered with only the tiniest scrap of lace to constitute a morning cap, held no hint of gray. Her face owned not a single wrinkle, of that she was certain, for she inspected it in her mirror throughout each day. But the lady was no fool. Time was running out for her to improve her circumstances before the passing years marred her looks.

Schooling her features into one of delight, she cooed, "Why, Lord Hargrove, I did not expect to see you this morning, although I must say it is always a pleasure when you come to my little house."

The viscount stood at one of the windows, gazing out into the garden with rapt attention and seemed not to heed a single word the lady said. "I say, Lady W, is that girl in the garden your *little* stepdaughter? She is quite the beauty and looks old enough to be presented."

Lucinda knew a sudden urge to scream. Why had

Fate punished her so with a stepchild? And one who was so disobedient. Forcing her clenched fists to relax and taking a calming breath, she casually stepped to the window beside his lordship. That wretched girl was likely to ruin everything. "Why, so it is." She lowered her voice. "It is a sad fact that the girl shall never make her bow to Society. She is prone to . . . well, spells that quite frighten the servants, so I am forced to keep her confined to the garden much of the time." The blatant lie rolled off her tongue with ease.

Hargrove's leathery face puckered thoughtfully. "Damned shame, that. Why, she's quite the most beautiful creature I've ever set eyes upon. You could have fired her off even without a dowry."

A glittering look of anger settled in Lucinda's green eyes at the compliment to Sarah. "Indeed, I had no idea you were so taken with dark locks, sir." She turned her back on the pastoral scene of the girl sitting in the shaded arbor, the small pink and white flowers entwined in the arched trellis, framing the girl like a painting.

The gentleman, unaware of the jealousy he'd set loose in the lady's breast, said, "Well, like most men, I suppose I'm as struck by a pretty face as the next, no matter the hair color."

In an even frostier tone, Lucinda replied, "Just so." Without another word, she moved away from the window as thoughts of punishment for Sarah swirled about in her head. At the fireplace she turned to study the man, who continued to stare at her stepdaughter as if moonstruck.

Viscount Hargrove was nearing fifty and not the least bit handsome. His gray hair was thinning while his waist appeared to expand with each year. He owned no fashion sense, dressing the part of a gen-

tleman farmer with black leather buckskins which
had seen many a cleaning, a dark green suede vest
which needed a good cleaning and a loose-fitted
brown coat many years out of fashion. He was twice
widowed, with an aging invalid mother who, rumor
held, ruled her son with an iron hand. All these
elements together made the gentleman an unlikely
marriage prospect for most, but the one thing that
made him attractive to Lucinda was that he possessed a fortune separate from his entailed estate.
She'd made a mistake with Whitefield. All she had
received after the baron's death was a mere pittance
to live on in this stuffy dower house plus a stepchild
who was a monstrous burden.

With a determined pat of her golden curls and
remembering what was at stake, she reined in her
ill temper. In her sweetest voice, she called, "My
dear Lord Hargrove, do come away from the window and tell me to what I owe the pleasure of this
visit."

He reluctantly dropped the curtain and moved
to the woman who'd been the object of his visit.
"Spells, you say," he repeated as if he couldn't draw
his thoughts from the girl in the garden. "Is there
nothing Dr. Sparks can do for the chit?"

Scarcely able to manage a civil tone, Lucinda
snapped, "Not a thing."

"Pity." Having put two wives in the ground, Hargrove was not unfamiliar with female whims and
what he saw in the lady's face brought him out of
his muse. "But then I did not come to pester you
with questions about the child. I think what you
need is a drive about the countryside, my dear.
Brought my curricle for just such an outing."

"Why, that is indeed what I need on such a lovely
day. Allow me to send for my bonnet and gloves."

Looking up at the gentleman through her lashes, she said, "It is always such a delight to be driven by a notable whip." With that the lady left the gentleman.

Hargrove wandered back to the window. Drawing back the sheer curtain, he again surveyed the chit in the garden. "Such a pity." With one final sigh, he strode out of the room.

Out in the garden, Sarah continued to pen her letter to Ella, unaware that she had been the object of discussion in the drawing room, and that she would be punished for having left the rear garden. She had been nearly a month home, if one could call what her stepmother provided such, and life had fallen into something of a routine. Her mornings were spent in the kitchen with Cook, helping where the old woman would allow. Afternoons she read or did needlework, and evenings she joined her stepmother at dinner when the widow didn't go out to join friends. That was the way the lady preferred it, claiming her nerves could not handle the noise and fuss of a young female before three in the afternoon.

Sarah laughed at that thought. It was not as if she were sliding down the banister or swinging from the chandelier in the drawing room like a wild child. She hadn't even been so wicked when she was much younger. Yet she was not heartbroken to be denied her ladyship's company. She was far happier teaching Cook new recipes, helping out in the stillroom, or gathering flowers from the rear garden for the front hall.

What her stepmother did with her days, Sarah was uncertain. She often heard the sounds of carriages coming and going, but she was never summoned to meet any of Lady Whitefield's friends. Many afternoons the lady went out to pay calls, but again there was no invitation for her stepdaughter to join her. On the evenings she stayed in, there were only complaints and criticisms for Sarah to suffer. Nothing she did ever pleased Lucinda.

With a sigh, Sarah went back to describing her life to Ella, who unlike Rose, would very well understand. She'd not heard from her friends, but she knew it was early days yet, and no doubt it would be difficult for Ella to find someone to frank her letters. Luckily for Sarah, the new Lord Whitefield had offered that service when he'd stopped by during her first week back from school. She'd received a scold from Lucinda for having been in the front hall at his arrival, but it had been worth the trimming to acquire the gentleman's generosity with his franking privilege.

The May air grew pleasantly warm and the hum of the bees in the flowers above her encouraged Sarah to lean back and enjoy the quiet solitude. While this isolation was not of her choosing, her life was not entirely unpleasant.

"Pardon me, Miss Sarah," a voice called from the edge of the garden.

Sarah looked up to see the tousled gray curls of Brinkman, the butler, as he poked his head out the drawing room window. It was most irregular for a servant not to come out to her, but she'd known him since childhood, and age made it difficult for him to come up and down the stairs that led to the garden.

"There's a gentleman to see you, child."

Sarah's blue eyes widened. "A gentleman? Are you certain he wishes to see me?" She didn't know any gentleman. For a moment, visions of a handsome young man swirled in her head, then she realized she had grown fanciful in her loneliness. She had no such gentleman in her acquaintance and therefore couldn't have such an enticing caller.

"I may be old, Miss Sarah, but I ain't gone dotty yet. 'Twas Miss Sarah Whiting he requested to see. Hurry, child. Don't keep him waiting."

She set her small portable secretaire on the bench and hurried across the garden to the rear entrance, which she'd been instructed to use. Out of breath as she reached the hallway, she stopped a moment to smooth down her hair, which she still wore loose with only a white ribbon to hold it back from her face. Her stepmother had failed to offer her the services of a maid, so Sarah had to make do and often only bushed out the tangles.

Brinkman stood beside the parlor door, and winked at her as he swept it open and announced in a formal baritone, "Miss Sarah Whiting."

Sarah almost giggled at his austere countenance, then she straightened and entered the room with all the decorum she'd been taught at Miss Parson's. To her disappointment, the gentleman proved to be a plump, middle-aged man with thinning brown hair combed forward to cover his balding pate. He was dressed in varying shades of black, the coat being older than his waistcoat and pantaloon. His loosely tied white cravat and his white stockings were the exception to his dark attire. He reminded her of a shopkeeper or vicar with his staid manner, but as she looked closer, she could see humor reflected in the gray eyes that surveyed her with interest.

"Good morning, Miss Whiting. I hope I find you well." When she acknowledged that she was, he continued. "I am Albert Cornell, solicitor to the late Miss Phoebe Whiting, your father's aunt."

Sarah searched her memory, but she could remember nothing of the lady. Uncertain what to say, she suggested, "Do be seated, sir, and tell me how I might help you."

The gentleman chuckled as he waited for Sarah to sit, then he took the seat opposite her. "I think I am the one come to help you, my dear girl." He opened a black valise and drew several documents from within. "I have come to inform you that your great-aunt has made you the sole recipient of her estate."

Sarah sat speechless for a moment, her mind in a whirl at the possibilities. Then her conscience got the better of her. "Mr. Cornell, I must confess that I do not know any Aunt Phoebe."

"Very likely, Miss Whiting, for my client was stricken with smallpox while you were but a infant, and she rarely left her house in Rye where she settled on inheriting from her aunt. But that did not mean she was unaware of you." He smiled at her, then pulled a pair of spectacles from his pocket and set them upon his nose. "Now, child, there is a great deal of legal stuff here, but what is most important to you is that—"

The door to the drawing room flew open and Lucinda swept into the room. Her cheeks were flushed pink, but whether from her drive or at finding a man with her stepdaughter was uncertain. "What is the meaning of this, Sarah? Who is this man? Sir, I demand that you tell me what you are doing closeted with my stepdaughter."

The man rose, bowing. "My lady, I am a solicitor come to bring Miss Whiting good news."

"Solicitor." The word seemed to conjure all kinds of ideas in the lady's head. A look of pure cunning transformed her ladyship's face for a moment, then seeming to remember herself, she gestured for the man to again be seated as she sat beside Sarah. "Well, sir, it seems that it would have been more ethical for you to have informed me of whatever you must tell Sarah, for, after all, I am her guardian."

The solicitor peered at the lovely widow with sage old eyes. "In the normal course of matters, I would have, madam, but due to the unusual nature of this will, I deemed it not necessary."

"Indeed," Lady Whitefield intoned in her haughtiest voice. "I believe I am the best judge of that. Pray tell me what you have come to say."

The gentleman cleared his throat. "Miss Phoebe Whiting, aunt of the late Lord Whitefield, has left the bulk of her fortune to Miss Sarah Whiting. The estate is in excess of thirty thousand pounds." There was the tiniest gasp from the widow before the gentleman continued. "The funds are to be held in trust for the young lady until she reaches the age of five-and-twenty."

"She is not to have a single penny until then? Why that is over six years away." Lady Whitefield rose and began to pace back and forth, stopping briefly to absently pat at her curls in front of the large looking glass beside the doorway. It was only one of several that hung on the walls of the room. "Those funds would do a great deal to improve our . . . I mean her circumstances at present. You cannot know how difficult it is to make ends meet on the pittance we were left by her father since the estate was entailed."

Mr. Cornell took off his glasses, folded them, and put them in his pocket. "I fear there is nothing I can do, madam. Miss Phoebe was emphatic that the girl was not to receive a penny of her inheritance until her majority, or unless she marries."

Her ladyship came to stand facing the man, and

shook her finger at him. "Well, she could not have been familiar with our circumstances, or she would have seen that we need the money at once."

Cornell's eyes narrowed a bit. "Oh, I think I can be certain that Miss Phoebe was well informed about Miss Sarah's circumstances."

Lady Whitefield turned and once again paced. Her ill temper at the turn of events evident to all. At last seeming to get control of her emotions, she turned to her stepdaughter. "Well, child," she said in a sweet voice Sarah had never heard before, "I think you have had enough excitement for one morning. Perhaps you had better retire to your room. I shall see Mr. Cornell out."

Sarah, still reeling from this sudden unexpected good fortune, did not argue with her stepmother. She rose, but the solicitor halted her and requested her signature on several documents. After that, the girl bid the gentleman and her stepmother good day. Mr. Cornell promised to keep in touch, then as the widow moved to open the door, he whispered to the young lady that she might apply to him for an advance anytime, should the need arise.

Shutting the door behind Sarah, Lady Whitefield advanced on the gentleman. "Sir, pray tell me all there is to know about this inheritance. As Sarah's guardian, I must be fully informed."

With a sigh, the solicitor gestured to the opposite seat and settled down to give the widow the particulars of the will. Some thirty minutes later as Lady Whitefield stood before the looking glass of the drawing room, listening to Mr. Cornell's carriage departing, she smiled at her reflection. As the man had droned on and on, a plan had popped into Lucinda's mind. It was a bit drastic, but after all, the ends justified the means did they not?

She rang for the maid, then told her to send for the head groom.

"Barlow, my lady? In the house?" The maid took a step back her eyes widening.

"Don't behave as if I requested you to summon a savage wolf, girl. He may look a bit forbidding, but one cannot be faulted for the face God gives one. The man has been with my family since I was a little girl, and I would trust him with my life." With that she turned her back on the foolish servant, who hurried from the room.

Lucinda's attachment to the strange-looking man had always puzzled most who knew her, but to her ladyship, he stood as the one person who always did her bidding without question. He had saved her as a girl from a fire at her family home near Dorchester and never told she was the one who set the fire in a pique at her father for refusing to buy her a new pony. Henceforth, she'd believed he was her protector, while he adored her golden beauty with the devotion of a puppy.

The dowager moved to the window and settled in a chair, arranging her skirts just so. Then she drew out her handkerchief and prepared to play her part well.

Barlow entered the room after a knock, drawing his battered felt hat from his head. Well into his fifties, the years had done little to improve his appearance, for now his gray hair was frizzy and flew about his head like some demented soul's. The lines etched in his sun-browned skin had settled into great folds, giving him the look of an ancient troll come to life.

"Ye be wantin' me, my lady?"

"Oh, Barlow, whatever am I to do with that dreadful girl?" She dabbed at her eyes, then gave him a look of entreaty.

The old man's thick brows drew together. "Is the young miss misbehavin'? Ye should send her away again, my lady. Ye can't be lettin' her destroy yer peace."

"I cannot or everyone will think *me* a bad person. They will not know what she has put me through, only that I did not take my late husband's daughter to my heart. But I do believe she will put me in an early grave with her wickedness." She put her head in her hands and her shoulders shook as if she were utterly distraught.

Despite his age, Barlow straightened to his full six-and-a-half-foot height. "Why, I'll see the baggage dead afore I'll let that happen, my lady."

Lucinda lift her tear-free face and smiled up at him. "I knew I could count on my dear Barlow."

His eyes widened a moment with dawning realization. With a resigned grunt and a nod of his head, he patted her shoulder. "Ye leave things to me. Yer problem shall disappear."

Without another word, the groom left the drawing room as if he had much on his mind. Lady Whitefield bounded up from her chair and dashed across to the looking glass beside the door. She grinned at her reflection. "Beauty *and* money, why I shall be the Toast of London by the autumn." On that happy thought she retired to her room to change and make plans.

Severe rain buffeted the county of Shropshire for several days following Mr. Cornell's visit, but little else changed in Sarah's life. Her stepmother was only slightly more civil without an audience to see her performance, making the young girl realize that six years was a very long time to await her freedom.

With no one else to turn to, she sat in the kitchen, seeking Cook's advice about what best to do while she waited to receive her inheritance. "Do you think I might apply to be a governess? Miss Parson had me teach piano and voice whenever Miss Ritter was ill with the ague last year and I quite liked the task."

Cook looked up from the dough she kneaded and laughed. "Certain I am you'd do very well with teachin', miss. But there's not a lady in her right mind as would hire a pretty young thing like yourself to be distractin' her husband."

Sarah sighed and began to draw pictures in the flour that had spilled across the table. "Then should I be a companion to some older lady?"

Pressing the finished dough into a pan, Cook shook her head. "Child, there are worse things than being ignored by Lady Whitefield. If you take my advice, you'll stay here and do the things that proper young ladies do to while away your days— read, walk, sew, and tolerate her ladyship's oddities. The time will slip by much faster than you think. Besides, didn't you say that solicitor offered you an advance on your funds? Write the fellow and see what he—"

At that moment the service bell jingled for the drawing room. Cook called to Betty in the laundry room. "Go see what her ladyship wants. She must be havin' guests today to be out of her room so early."

After the girl left, Cook folded her arms across her ample breasts, looking straight at her young mistress. "Take my advice and give the matter a great deal of thought before you decide. You don't want to end up in a situation far worse than this. It would make six years seem like twenty."

Sarah came round the table and hugged the older woman. "I will, Maggie, I promise."

Within minutes the thin servant with a water-stained apron returned. "Lady Whitefield wants you at once, miss."

Sarah looked at the clock above the kitchen fireplace. "Whatever can this be about? She never wishes to see me before seven in the evening."

"You'll only know after you've seen her, child." Cook make a shooing gesture with her hands.

Sarah hurried up the stairs to the drawing room, where she discovered her stepmother dressed in a fashionable blue afternoon gown with a navy spencer, her navy high-crown bonnet trimmed with white lace. She was seated in front of a fire that had been set to take the dampness out of the room. Sarah saw no point in mentioning the fact that she'd had no fire in her bedchamber this morning when it would have been greatly appreciated. "Good afternoon, Mama." She curtsied then took the seat opposite her stepmother.

"Ah, Sarah. I have decided we must do something about your wardrobe." The widow's gaze scrutinized the plain gray gown, and she gave a slight shudder.

Sarah frowned. "But you said there was no need when I came back from school."

"There was no need when you had no dowry." Lady Whitefield smiled, but her eyes remained cool. "You are about to become an heiress, so your chances for a good marriage have greatly improved."

Looking down at the much-hated school dress,

Sarah sighed with pleasure. "I should like that very much."

Lady Whitefield rose and walked to a nearby table and retrieved her navy calfskin gloves. "As I knew you would. But I fear I am much occupied with friends this afternoon, so I have ordered Barlow to accompany you to Montford to have your measurements taken by Mrs. Trudeau, the local seamstress. I should like to have at least one gown done by Friday so that I may take you to meet Lady Hart, who is just returned from Town."

Sarah's gaze flew to the rain-flecked window. "But if you have the carriage, how shall I reach the . . ." Her voice trailed off, for she knew what was to come.

The widow ceased drawing on her final glove, her beautiful face set in a haughty mask. "You may walk. The rain has nearly stopped. Are you going to be missish about a few sprinkles?"

"No, Mama," Sarah said, meekly. Yet her gaze returned to the dark sky looming in the drawing room windows. She knew better than to protest the situation, or she might lose her promised treat. What was a bit of a damp walk in comparison to a new wardrobe? On that thought she rose and bid her stepmama good day before going upstairs to retrieve her bonnet and cloak.

The head groom awaited her on the steps of the dower house, looking even more menacing than she remembered. She greeted him softly, but for her efforts all she got was an unintelligible grunt before he stalked off toward Montford, splashing though the puddles as if he didn't see them.

The dower cottage lay some two miles beyond the River Severn from the village of Montford. Barlow set a rapid pace. Sarah had to nearly run to keep up with him and avoid the great puddles of water dotting the road. The rain had stopped, but the air was heavy with the possibility of more to come from the darkening clouds.

Intent on keeping her skirts dry, Sarah ran straight into the back of Barlow when he stopped suddenly. "Oh, I do beg your pardon." She looked up to see what had made the groom come to such a sudden stop, only to see that the rain-swollen river had overflowed its bank. The top of the bridge could be seen, but the roadway was several inches deep in water.

"Oh, dear, we shan't be able to go to Montford today," Sarah said, disappointed.

"Nonsense," Barlow barked and without a by-your-leave, swept Sarah into his arms and began to trudge through the water.

As they approached the center of the bridge that had stood for hundreds of years, Sarah gazed up-river, and her heart froze. The days of heavy spring rains had turned the Severn into a rushing torrent, filled with uprooted trees and overburdened limbs that had fallen during the storm. The debris rushed along with the river's current at a frightening speed, thumping against the bridge's stone pillars. She could feel Barlow struggling through the deepening water and wondered if they would be able to return home tonight. Where would they—

That thought was left unfinished when suddenly, without the least warning, Barlow veered to the bridge's balustrade and tossed Sarah into the middle of the rushing river. She shrieked as she plunged toward the surging waters. The strangled cry was silenced as her head sank below the surface. She thought herself about to die. Why had he thrown her in the water? But she had no time to ponder the question as she fought against the river's deadly pull.

Sarah's lungs seemed about to burst when she realized that her hated gray gown had snagged on something that was preventing her from sinking any further even as she was being carried along on the swift current. She struggled to pull herself to the surface. After what seemed an eternity, she thrust her head out of the water, and gasped in sweet air. She wrapped her arm around the rapidly moving uprooted tree that had saved her life.

In shock at the strange turn of events, her mind seemed not to work. Then she knew she must take action to save herself. Attempting to get her bearings, she looked about, but all she saw was the fast-moving landscape the river coursed through. She turned and stared back at where she'd been, but a sharp angle in the river kept her from seeing the Montford Bridge or Barlow. She was a far cry from being safe. All she could do was hang on to the log and pray that she might eventually be able to work her way to shore.

Once again it began to rain, but in her situation it didn't matter, for she could hardly become wetter. Her arms began to ache from clinging so desperately to the rough tree. Several times she shouted for help as she moved past small towns or lone cottages near the river's edge, but all the residents were indoors due to the inclement weather. No one came to her rescue.

The storm made darkness fall early, and Sarah knew she had to do something to get out of the river or she would eventually be swept out to sea, if she could hold on for that long. She'd never learned to swim, but she'd often seen several small boys playing in the creek near Miss Parson's. They'd kicked their legs and propelled themselves across the water. Her own limbs were stiff and cold, but she tried moving them as best she could and discovered the awkward motion moved her closer to the shoreline, for there was no visible bank in the swollen river.

For what seemed like hours she kicked, yet the vagaries of the river seemed to be working against her, randomly swirling her away from the bank. She would have to rest at intervals before she resumed the seemingly futile task, for the river was much wider than normal. Complete darkness soon overtook her, but she was determined to reach dry land. After several strong kicks, her feet touched bottom in a small nook in the river. Relief flooded Sarah, but she was too tired to think about anything but climbing out of the cold water. Her legs seemed not to want to hold her as the water grew more shallow. Falling to her hands and knees, she crawled her way up to a small hillock before collapsing, sweet grass pressed against her cheek. Her eyes closed, and she knew she had to rest, before she attempted to make her way back home. With that she fell into an exhausted slumber.

Wild Rose Cottage's gardens were only a small part of its beauty. Constructed of granite with a thatched roof, the building seemed to own some magical quality when the sun lit the mullioned windows, giving the house a warm and enticing glow. It was an elegant little house that sat on a small rise some one hundred yards from the River Severn. The red and white roses, more tended by nature than man, seemed to grow everywhere.

Built by the second Earl of Longmire for his mistress some two hundred years prior, it had become one of the more profitable buildings on Longmire's estate after that lady's death. Often travelers who journeyed past the neat little structure on the road to Shrewsbury would inquire in the town if the residence might be let. Presently all the locals knew was that a family named Ward had set up housekeeping some six months before, albeit one saw little of the residents save the children and, on occasion, an old servant.

On the morning after the worst storm that spring, Jamie Ward pushed open the front parlor window and leaned out. At twelve he was the eldest of the seven children of Captain John Ward and his wife, Cassandra. The lad was handsome, with raven's wing black hair, cut neatly about his ears, and twinkling blue eyes that surveyed the river's edge with interest. Taking a deep breath of the clean air, he announced over his shoulder, "The rain has ceased and the river seems to be going down as well. It looks like it shall be a sunny day."

Behind him ten-year-old Ronald stood peering into an empty box he held in his hand, a frown marring his youthful face. His appearance was much like his brother's, but his eyes were more gray than blue and he had already passed Jamie in height. "That is good because we are out of willow bark." Unlike Jamie, Ronald was a serious young lad, with a penchant for science, and his mien seemed older than his elder brother's.

Drawing back inside, Jamie frowned, an unusual expression for the normally cheerful boy. "Is Mark very ill?"

Ronald closed the box. "I think he only has a cold. His fever is down this morning."

Jamie patted his brother's shoulder. "You've done

a wonderful job of taking care of the boys. I think you'll make an excellent physician someday. And don't fret so, everything will work out . . . somehow."

Before Ronald could respond, eight-year-old Adam Ward strolled into the parlor, the family dog, Percy, a brown-and-white bearded collie, at his side. Dark brown curls hung about the boy's thin face, and his deep blue eyes reflected impatience. "When are we going to eat? Breakfast is always late since Philly left," he complained, glaring at Jamie.

Despite his brother's peevish mood, the older boy smiled. "Is everyone up and dressed?"

Adam nodded, even as he curiously eyed the box Ronald held. "The others are waiting in the dining room. Peter is watching after them."

Jamie rolled his eyes at that bit of news, for putting Peter in charge was a bit like setting the child to watch the adult. Jamie led the way toward where the rest of the children waited. "I have everything prepared." He greeted the four younger children seated at the table: nine-year-old Peter, Adam's twin Alan, and the youngest ones, Luther and Mark, all waiting with restless anticipation. All dark-haired and well-featured, they made a handsome tableau. Jamie passed through the rear door into the kitchen, calling for them to be patient. Within minutes he returned with a tray laden with sliced bread, butter, and apricot jam as well as a pitcher of milk. Most of the boys reached for slices, and began to butter them as they liked, but Jamie helped Mark, as Ronald helped Luther, for these were the youngest at five and six, and the family didn't have butter or jam to waste.

Ronald gave Luther his buttered bread then

grabbed a cup of milk and took a large gulp before he asked, "What about the willow bark?"

Licking a smear of butter off his thumb after he handed the prepared slice to Mark, Jamie said, "We'll go after breakfast. I used to help Philly when he gathered it for Mama. I know where to find it and what to do."

A hush fell over the table for a moment. Mark looked up at Jamie. "I miss Mama." There was a murmur of agreement.

"We all do, little brother." He ruffled the youngest's black hair. "Finish your breakfast."

Alan, Adam's identical twin, put down his bread. "Well, I miss Phillips as well. Do you think he'll come back?"

Jamie and Ronald exchanged a telling look over the children's heads. They had discussed what might have happened to the old man and the possibility of his return, but neither held much hope, for Philly would never have abandoned them voluntarily. Jamie put on a brave face for Alan. "I hope Philly will find his way back, somehow." But his tone held little confidence that their lone servant would return. The man had gone to town three weeks earlier and had never returned. The two eldest sat down and partook of the meager breakfast.

After a hurried meal, Jamie rose. "Adam, take the others into the back parlor and read them a story."

"I don't see why I always have to be the one to take care of the others. Let Peter do it or better yet let us all go look for bark. I want to go out," Adam grumbled.

Little Mark nodded agreement. "Me too." Then he sneezed.

Ronald hurried round the table and felt his brother's forehead. With a relieved sigh he announced, "No fever. And no going out today for you."

"Peter is going with us," Jamie announced. He didn't add that while Peter was older than the twins, he was the least responsible of the lot. "It is too muddy just yet for the rest of you to be outside."

Alan yawned as if he'd gotten up too early, then gestured at the little ones. "We cannot all go out with Mark sick. The little ones can play spillikins instead of a story. I'll just rest on the sofa." Without a backward glance he led Mark and Luther from the dining room.

Jamie quirked a brow at Adam. "It's going to be very muddy where we'll be going."

The boy looked down at the only boots he was likely to have for a long time. Then making a face, he said, "Oh, very well, I shall stay and play with the boys." With that ungracious announcement, Adam marched from the room in a huff.

Ronald, Jamie, and Peter went to the kitchen door and pulled on their boots. They called to Percy to come for his morning run and headed out toward the river road.

The great hairy dog bounded well ahead of the boys, but his brown-and-white fur could easily be spotted as he dashed in and out of the green foliage, stopping to sniff the ground on occasion as if he were pursuing prey. Peter chattered about the possibility of mythological creatures living in the woods surrounding the cottage and claimed that was what Percy was hunting. Ronald snickered and Jamie declared his brother quite daft.

They arrived at a cluster of willows situated on a rise beside the Severn, and Jamie showed his brothers how to harvest the bark. The older boys worked diligently, but Peter, soon distracted by Percy's barking, wandered off to see what the dog had found.

Within minutes, Peter's shouts echoed on the morning air. "Jamie! Ronnie! Hurry! I've found a dead body!"

The two older boys exchanged a puzzled glance. Peter could be harebrained and nonsensical, but even he wouldn't tease about something like that. They put down their knives and hurried further down the river, where they could hear Percy still yapping. They halted in amazement as they passed a clump of small fir trees. There on the ground was a soaking wet woman who obviously had crawled out of the river before collapsing.

Moving closer, Jamie could see her gown was muddy, her hair tangled and matted with twigs and other debris. What struck him the most was how very still she lay and how very pale her skin was. A chill raced down his spine. He'd never touched a dead person; Philly had done everything to prepare their mother for burial. But Jamie knew he would have to touch this one to see if she still lived or had drowned.

To his surprise, Ronald stepped up to the body. Kneeling, he turned her over without the least bit of hesitation. He placed his hand against her throat, then his gray eyes widened. "She's not dead. But very likely she will be if we don't take her somewhere warm and dry."

Peter stooped and brushed her black hair away from her face. "She's very pretty, I think. Just what a mermaid would look like, only with a fish's tail." He looked to Jamie. "Should I run and fetch Dr. Bergen?"

Being the eldest, the decision was his, but Jamie was torn. Should he risk this unknown female's life, or that of his brothers? It was the hardest choice he'd had to make since their mother's death, but he would do what he must. "No, we'll take her back to the cottage. Ronnie can take care of her. We cannot have Dr. Bergen asking any questions."

Ronald stood up. "Are you sure? I've only got Mama's herbal book to go by. What if the lady becomes worse?"

Jamie stared into the lady's pale face. He nipped on his lip with indecision. At last he looked at his brother. "If she isn't any better by tomorrow I'll send Peter for the doctor then. We'll just have to think of something to explain things, should Bergen question us."

"Good." Ronald appeared relieved that all the responsibility for the ailing woman wouldn't be on his young shoulders. "Peter, run back to the house and bring a blanket. Also have the others come as well. It will likely take all of us to carry her."

Peter dashed off with Percy at his heels.

Jamie knelt, taking her hand, which was icy despite the growing warmth of the day. "How do you think she came to be in the water?"

Ronald shrugged. "The river has been flooding for days. We've seen all sorts of things floating past. Who knows?" Then his eyes widened. "Jamie, what if someone comes looking for her?"

Jamie rose and looked up and down the river. Thankfully there was no one in sight. "We must hide her in the cottage as soon as possible. We don't want a lot of people coming round."

Scarcely ten minutes passed before the remaining Ward brothers came running up the path, following Peter, all agog at what they'd been told. Jamie shushed them, reminding them they didn't want to draw attention to themselves. They must hurry and get the unconscious woman out of sight.

With Ronald taking charge, they quickly rolled the lady onto the blanket. There was no chatter or speculation about her, only quiet determination to take her to the cottage as quickly as possible. Finally they arrived at Wild Rose and breathed a collective sigh of relief.

Jamie ordered, "We must put her in Mama's room."

Opening the door of the room, which most hadn't entered in nearly two months, they slid their burden on the bed, then Ronald began barking orders for dry linens, warm bricks, and toweling. While the younger ones hied about doing their part to assist, Jamie went to the front parlor window and looked about. They had done it. They'd gotten her inside with no one being the wiser. Their secret was still safe.

Two

Over a hundred miles south of where the Ward brothers had pulled Miss Whiting from the river, the owner of Wild Rose Cottage was on a mission of some urgency. Former Captain Titus Lindon stood on the front steps of Beaumont Hall and handed the butler his card. "Longmire to see Sir Evan." The masterful tone was at odds with the earl's youthful face.

Jarvis, twenty years in the Beaumont's service, took the engraved vellum without excessive deference for the London swell before him and announced, "I regret to say that my master is not at home to visitors at present, my lord."

Titus tipped his black beaver back on his golden curls, giving him a rakish appearance as he produced a devilish grin. "Oh, I'm certain he will see me, my good man. Owes me a debt, he does, and a gentleman always honors his debts."

A thoughtful expression settled into the gray-haired servant's eyes as they swept the gentleman from his fashionable curls to the tips of his white-topped Hessians. Nothing in the earl's appearance was reassuring. Much of his attire was the first stare of fashion, yet the gentleman had fallen victim to some of the more radical modes of style such as oversized gold buttons on his riding coat and an overabundance of decorative fobs dangling at his waist. The bright green kerseymere garment framed a starched cravat so high that the points of his shirt give the young man's head only minimal mobility. A Town Tulip without a doubt. But there could be no arguing with his statement, and Jarvis opened the door wider. "Mayhap you should speak with Sir Evan's sister, Mrs. Sorley, my lord?"

The butler led the Earl of Longmire to a drawing room, an elegant chamber done in subtle shades of gold and green with gilt furniture. He strolled to the window to survey the gardens and determined that his old army friend had inherited a neat and well-cared-for property. It gave him confidence to ask the favor that he intended to request, for only a man of property would understand his dilemma. Within minutes the lady joined him.

Mrs. Agnes Sorley was one of those no-nonsense females who can be so handy in a crisis, but in most other social situations are quite abrupt. Tall and rotund, she nearly dwarfed the earl. She was dressed in a lavender muslin gown with no frills save a small white collar, giving her the appearance of a housekeeper. It struck the earl that in fact she might be enacting the part for her bachelor brother. She owned none of Sir Evan's features save his deep green eyes, but they were nearly obscured in the folds of her round cheeks.

"Lord Longmire, I am Mrs. Sorley. I do believe Jarvis informed you my brother is not receiving company at the moment. He is not fully recovered from his wounds as you, of all people, should well know." Her tone was almost one of a parent speaking to a naughty child.

"My dear madam, I do apologize for barging in

on you in such a manner, but I had a disturbing report about my old friend from Colonel Preston. He seemed to think that Sir Evan suffered from melancholia more than his wounds."

"I cannot think how the colonel should have come to such a conclusion after a conversation of no more than five minutes. My brother will rally soon, if only his old regiment would leave him in peace. His army days are quite at an end what with his responsibilities here and the nature of his injuries. These visits only tend to promote discontent, my lord." The lady folded her hands in front of her, seeming to feel that was a sufficient dismissal.

Titus might be a new earl, having inherited scarcely three months earlier at the death of his brother, but he well knew how to wield the power of his station. Looking down his nose at Mrs. Sorley, he coolly announced, "I intend to see my friend, madam—with or without your leave for I bring tidings from the Prince Regent."

"Why did you not say that in the first place, sir? Follow me." Exhibiting no softening in her objections to the gentleman's intrusion, she turned and led the way into the hall, past several doors. After a knock and without waiting for permission, she opened the door to what appeared to be a darkened library. She gestured for his lordship to enter then shut the door with a snap behind him.

From near the fireplace a quarrelsome voice barked, "Go away, Aggie. Can you not find sufficient tasks to keep you occupied so that you needn't intrude upon my solitude?"

The earl moved to where he could make out a pair of long booted legs stretched out from a wing-backed chair. "Is that any way to greet the man who saved your life at Toulouse, old friend?"

"Titus." There was no pleasure in Sir Evan's tone, nor did he rise to welcome his visitor. He merely stared with red-shot eyes at the unwelcome sight.

Hoping to delay a dismissal, the earl moved to one of the windows. He took a great liberty and drew back the curtains, flooding the room with light. On turning back to his friend, he struggled to hide the shock he experienced. Sir Evan Beaumont was a pale imitation of the man Titus had known in the Peninsula. His auburn hair had grown long and unruly. The tanned face in the earl's memory had been replaced by a gaunt pallor with several days' growth of auburn stubble, the fresh saber scars healed but bright red. His crisp regimental jacket, supplanted by a rumpled lawn shirt open at the collar and looking as if it had seen several days' use. In one hand, the gentleman held an empty glass, and the strong odor of brandy permeated the library.

This was worse than Titus had expected. His old friend had been the consummate military man, a prize for any regiment. Even in his darkest moments, Sir Evan, a career soldier, had taken the surgeon's news in Toulouse that his wounds would make it impossible to continue in his chosen profession in a stoic manner. On that faithful day, Titus had experienced little fear that his friend would not rally and return home to the normal, if somewhat tranquil life, of a gentleman farmer.

That had been nearly five months ago but Fate had not finished dealing the baronet more bad turns. On his arrival home, it seemed that Miss Violet Hall, his fiancée for over a year, had jilted him within a month to marry a viscount. News of such a scandal had reached even London Society.

It was perfectly clear to Titus that the loss of Beaumont's profession and his love had left him awash in despondency. Something had to be done. In a forced cheerful tone, the earl announced, "I bring Prinny's best wishes for your recovery and his desire to thank you for your heroic efforts in France."

Sir Evan sat his glass on the nearby table and eyed the brandy decanter for a moment. He evidently decided to delay a new glassful until after his friend departed. He leaned his head back against the leather chair and eyed his visitor cynically. "You didn't ride all this way for what could easily have been included in a letter."

Titus hesitated a moment. He had to be careful, or his plot to help his friend would go awry. And in truth he needed Sir Evan as much as the baronet needed something to drag him back from the depth of despair. Deciding that honesty would be best, he plunged into the heart of the problem. "Devil take me, Beau, I'm in something of a situation. I was hoping you might help me the way you did with that Spanish dancer in Lisbon."

Young and foolish upon his arrival in Portugal, Titus had pursued the beautiful Teresa de la Rosa, who danced nightly in one of the cantinas, unaware she was the mistress of the Marquez de Sousa. The hot-blooded Portuguese had sent seconds to look for the brash young captain. Learning of the danger, Sir Evan had Titus assigned to him as an exploring officer. Departing Lisbon posthaste, they'd spent months searching out French spies in the mountains. De Sousa's passion for revenge and the lady had waned by the time Titus returned to town, saving him from a musket ball or being sent home in disgrace for killing so important a man.

"Your penchant for the muslin set will be your

undoing." The baronet's tone sounded his disinterest.

"Not this time. She's a lady and she's agreed to be my wife. But her one request of me is, at present, beyond my ability."

A tiny spark of curiosity reflected in the shadows of the green eyes that surveyed the earl. "What is the lady's desire that you cannot fulfill?"

Titus settled in the chair opposite the baronet, but was silent for a moment as if gathering his thoughts. "I need to start at the source of my problem. You may remember that my father and I were estranged since my childhood when my mother took me and departed the estate. He saw no need for the so called 'spare,' feeling my older brother sufficient to fill his shoes. They both were virtual strangers to me. I had only the vaguest of memories of the estate when summoned from Vienna in March. I was informed that my father had been killed and my brother injured in a carriage accident. By the time I arrived at Longdale Hall, John was dead and I possessed no knowledge about what had taken place in the years of my absence. The estate books were a mess; my father's steward could only tell me that more had been taken from Longdale than invested back. It was clear to me that my father had not heeded much of Joiner's advice. John had no opportunity to do any damage or good to the estate, surviving my father by scarcely two weeks."

"I'm sorry for your loss, my friend. If it's money you need—"

Titus raised his hand. " 'Tis nothing like that. My mother left me well taken care of and, in truth, I didn't know my father or brother, so I feel only a modicum of loss at what might have been between

John and me, had he lived. The estate is the thing now since I plan to marry."

Sir Evan shrugged, then reached for the empty brandy glass. He turned the crystal stem between his fingers as if contemplating his next drink. "I cannot help with that, Titus. My own bailiff is an excellent manager. He has run this place with little advice from me since my own father passed. I'm a soldier; I can scarcely tell the difference between a turnip and a potato."

"Then it's just as well that I'm not staying to dine, for I cannot abide turnips." The earl grinned, but received a baleful stare from Sir Evan. In a hurried voice Titus continued. "This is something else entirely. I met Miss Georgina Fleming in Town when I was visiting my father's solicitor and it was love at first sight." He paused and his face took on a dreamy quality.

"My felicitations." Sir Evan's subdued tone brought Titus to his senses with the memory of the baronet's own recent disappointment at love.

Businesslike, the earl said, "Invited her and her family up to Shropshire while I set about putting the estate in good order. The long and the short of it is, she saw a particularly pretty cottage I have on my estate and nothing would do but that I put her mama and sisters there after we are married, since London is so far away. Her younger sister is sickly and only Georgiana can handle her when she has one of her spells, so it is imperative they be close by. I understood and I was perfectly willing, but now I stumbled across the strangest thing."

"The place is already let." Sir Evan was no fool, even if his mood was black. "I cannot see a problem. Explain to the present tenants and I am certain they will gladly vacate the premises. Good manners will allow nothing else."

Titus ran his hand through his blond hair, sending his curls into further disarray. "It's not leased. According to the terms of my father's will, this Ward creature has been given the right of tenancy for her life. Joiner, who met the woman on the occasion of her arrival, thinks she is some stage actress who captured my father's attention and somehow seduced him into giving her the cottage. Said he'd never seen the old earl so solicitous to a female before. When the steward pressed my father on the matter, he was told to mind his business, the woman was there to stay."

The baronet's red-rimmed gaze dropped to his dusty boots for a moment, then he looked back at the earl. "Then I think you should explain the facts to your fiancée."

"Tell the woman I'm about to marry that some light skirt is living in the best cottage on my estate? That my father was foolish enough to bring a common baggage and a passel of brats into his intimate circle of friends and family? There has to be another way." Titus pushed up from the chair and began to pace the library.

Sir Evan sat in silence as his friend continued to pace, offering no solution to the dilemma. The earl stopped at the window. "If only I hadn't . . ."

"Hadn't what?"

Titus turned but kept his gaze on his hands. "If only I hadn't promised Georgina that the cottage would be her mother's as soon as we returned from our honeymoon trip."

"That was foolish," Sir Evan stated, giving his friend no sway. Silence fell again, but soon he asked, "Have you considered offering Mrs. Ward a property of equal size somewhere else? I cannot think a stage actress would like living in the wilds of Shropshire indefinitely."

"I thought of that, but I cannot even speak with the creature. Those cursed children of hers practically slam the door in my face every time I try to speak with her, and Joiner has had no better luck. The messages I've left have been either ignored, or I'm told that the lady is too ill and cannot meet with me. I even lost my head and threatened her servant, Phillips, unless I spoke with the woman, which was stupid, for even he is playing least in sight."

Sir Evan put the brandy glass back on the table, and shook his head. "I see you have the same finesse you exhibited in Lisbon."

After a sheepish grin, Longmire's face settled into a puckered frown. "Perhaps I didn't exhibit the best judgment, but I tell you I've come to think there is something very havey-cavey going on at Wild Rose. The trouble is, my wedding is only a week away. Of course you are invited, for it's a very small affair at the estate due to my recent bereavements. But it means I haven't time to investigate before we depart."

He moved back to the seat opposite his friend, perching nervously on the edge of the brown leather. "That is where I was hoping you might be of some assistance."

"Me? What makes you think I shall have any better luck with the creature than you?" Auburn brows arched quizzically.

"Because she won't know there is a connection between us. Befriend her and find out all you can. You were the best strategist in our regiment. You always said, 'Know the enemy's weakness and make that your point of attack.' Give me what I need to remove this creature from that cottage, Beau. Or at the very least help me to understand why my father would have given the most valuable cottage on the estate to this woman rent-free."

Sir Evan's head began to shake. "I don't—"

"Pray, don't say no out of hand. I need you, old friend. Give the problem some thought." The earl rose, his face a study in supplication. "I truly mean her no harm even if she proves to be an actress, but I must have that cottage back for Georgina's family. You owe me this for Toulouse."

A thoughtful expression relaxed the lines of despondency on Sir Evan's face, making him look more his age. "It seems that you will have to stay and dine after all. I shall give you my answer after dinner."

With a smile, the earl shook his friend's good hand, an awkward business since it was his left. "I shall take a stroll about your gardens and leave you to make your decision."

Lord Longmire left Sir Evan wrestling with doubts. Should he involve himself in such a matter? Foremost in his mind was his debt to the man who'd risked his life to save him. He looked back at the brandy that had helped to numb the pain and disappointment about what life had heaped upon him, but he realized that would only cloud his mind. He would need his wits about him for such an important decision.

Two hours passed and Mrs. Sorley could contain herself no longer. What had the Earl of Longmire wanted with her brother? Messages from Prinny could only be an excuse to barge in, in her opinion. She certainly hoped that he hadn't come to put ideas in Evan's head, for she quite liked the way things had been since her brother's return. Why, she was practically in charge of Beaumont Hall like any true mistress of the manor. It was a far cry from the tiny house that Mr. Sorley had provided or her daughter's crowded manor, where she was made to feel like an intruder by her son-in-law.

A quick glance at the ormolu clock on the mantel told her she had the perfect excuse to invade his privacy. He rarely took tea in the afternoons, but she often inquired anyway. She put aside her knitting and slipped from the rear sitting room and down the hall. There were no servants in sight so she pressed an ear to the door. She heard not a word. Had the earl departed? That seemed unlikely for he'd come all the way from London.

Without further ado, she opened the door and halted in surprise. The library was bathed in the golden light of the late afternoon sun, all the curtains drawn open. She hadn't seen the room like this since before their father died. A movement drew her attention across the room. Her brother was seated behind the dark mahogany desk, but he appeared as idle as he had been since his return from France. Yet she detected a decided difference in him. It took several moments of study to realize pain and defeat had disappeared from his mein. In fact there was a determined jut of his chin as if he had some great plan in mind to undertake. Little tremors of worry niggled at her. Had the earl succeeded where others had failed in rallying Evan from his despair?

Her worried gaze swept the rest of the room, which was empty. "Did Longmire leave?"

Coming out of his brown study, Sir Evan replied, "He is in the garden awaiting my decision on a favor he requested." He eyed his sister thoughtfully, seeing her clearly for the first time since his return to Beaumont Hall. Did she always have such a look of discontent in her eyes? She'd never spoken of being unhappy here, but then women were secretive creatures. Violet had certainly fooled him completely. Her every letter had declared her love yet she'd run off and married another. The truth had come from her brother, who'd come to inform him that his scarred appearance had frightened her. Could Sir Evan blame her for turning her affections elsewhere, the gentleman had asked?

"What favor?" Mrs. Sorley's brows formed a flat line.

His sister's demand to hear of the earl's visit made him suddenly feel ungrateful for all she'd done. While he'd wallowed in self-pity like some green schoolboy, she'd taken over the duties of his household. No doubt she had made his life easier. Perhaps life had always been too easy for him. The loss of his career and the woman he was to marry within months had taken the wind from his sails in a way nothing else ever had. Well, all that was past and couldn't be changed, and it was time to face life anew, to do his duty. That dawning realization had struck him while looking into Titus's face as his friend dealt with the trials of a life he'd never expected.

"Lord Longmire wants me to go to Shropshire and handle a rather delicate matter for him."

"Go to Shropshire! In your condition?" The lady swelled with indignation, only adding to her porcinelike appearance. "Why, I would never have allowed him in the house had I any idea he would do anything so thoughtless." She bustled up to the desk and began repositioning the inkstand to suit her, a habit that had always driven Sir Evan to distraction. "You cannot be considering such a trip. Your right arm is still useless. Furthermore, have you forgotten that my daughter and the children are coming this week for a visit?"

The gentleman resisted the urge to groan. The apple had not fallen far from the tree in Mrs. Jane Sorley Watkins's case. His niece, like her mother, was forever wanting to make "small improvements" to the way things were done. Worse was the added disruption of two rambunctious boys and three noisy little girls, all utterly spoiled.

"Jane and the children do not come to see me, Aggie. Besides, I shall likely be gone only a few weeks. I'll attend Titus's wedding, then I shall handle matters in Shropshire and depart."

"But it would be the height of—"

The baronet rose abruptly, his left hand protectively cradling his nearly healed right hand in a steadying grip. "I have made my decision. I owe Titus much more than I can ever repay him for what he did for me. I leave in the morning. It will make no difference to your plans. Would you please ring for Jarvis and have him send Hawks to me at once?" He left his sister fuming in the library.

Some ten minutes later, Joshua Hawks, batman turned reluctant valet, arrived in Sir Evan's room. The baronet stood shirtless in front of a looking glass, surveying the damage done by a French saber. The actual scars were less shocking for the servant than the gaunt appearance of the man he'd served since Talavera. Hawks had always known pride in serving such a fine figure of a man, but he was convinced that his master had lost too much weight, a stone or more. What worried the valet more was Sir Evan's total indifference for anything but brandy since they'd returned to Beaumont and discovered the perfidy of his fiancée. Hawks had tried his best to interest the former major in matters on the estate, but only had his head nearly bitten off for his efforts.

"You sent for me, sir?"

The baronet turned and managed a halfhearted smile. "I am a sad sight, am I not?"

Hawks shrugged. " 'Tis nothing but what a few good meals wouldn't correct, sir."

Sir Evan ran his hand down the longer of the two scars over his chest. Like those marring his face, they were healed but remained red and tender. "I fear food cannot rid me of these."

"That's so, but time will make 'em fade. You won't even notice 'em. They are after all badges of honor, sir."

The gentleman chuckled. "I would have gladly foregone the honor. But I did not summon you to lament my condition. I fear I have overindulged in that for the past several months." He turned back to the looking glass. "We leave for the north. I want the curricle and my bays at the front door at six in the morning. I shall—"

"But, sir . . ." Hawks struggled not to smile, delighted at the news that his master once again would join the outside world. Only there was a major stumbling block. As Sir Evan turned to him, the valet stuttered, "I—I thought you knew. Mrs. Sorley sold the bays over a month ago."

"She what? My best team! Why, I should . . ." The gentleman's green eyes glinted with anger a moment, reminding Hawks of the glory days of battle, then the fire seemed to lower to only a small flame. "I suppose I have only myself to blame, but I can assure you there shall be changes made when I return."

Hawks couldn't resist a grin, for he'd known from the first that Mrs. Sorley found him wanting as a valet, and it would only have been a matter of time before he was discharged. But since the major had rallied to something of his old self, 'twould not be something he would have to worry his head about. Things would be quite different at Beaumont Hall in the future. "As to the carriage, sir, there are the grays."

"Then they shall have to do." Sir Evan lifted his injured right arm. "I'm not sure if I shall be able to manage a team, Hawks."

"It just wants a bit of use, sir. Besides, you won't be the first to learn to drive one-handed. I'll do some of the drivin', if need be. I hope there's no need for me to say that I'd drive you to Hades and back, sir."

"That is a bit far for our first outing. Shropshire will do." Sir Evan grinned as Hawks laughed. "For the present, shall we see if we can find me something that might fit me for dinner. Lord Longmire is joining us this evening." As an afterthought he added, "I think I shall stop in London and order some new clothes."

"Very good, sir." With that Hawks almost whistled a tune as he set about turning out his master in his most fashionable civilian attire, which was very difficult, for everything hung rather loosely on his frame, but a new wardrobe would soon remedy the problem. It was only a matter of time before Sir Evan Beaumont again looked like the gentleman Hawks had proudly served.

* * *

The musty odor of a room long closed filled
Sarah's consciousness as she came to her senses. She
snuggled into the comfort of the bed, vowing to give
her room a good cleaning, then memories of her
cold ride down the river flashed into her mind. Barlow had thrown her in the Severn! Her eyes flew
open and she sat up, remembering that she must
be miles from home. Where was she?

From the angle of the sunlight coming through
the windows, it was either very early or very late in
the day. She looked for a clock but found none. A
chill wracked her body, and she folded her arms
about her, only to realize she wore merely a chemise
and slip. She felt feverish and thirsty, her throat a
bit sore. Seeing a pitcher and glass on the nearby
night stand, she filled the tumbler with surprisingly
weak arms.

While she slaked her thirst, she took note of her
surroundings. There was nothing familiar about the
bedchamber. It was an ordinary room with heavy
oak furniture more suited to a larger room. Her
gaze swept the area, and she was struck by the
amount of dust on every surface. Even cobwebs
hung from the corners of the wooden framed can-
opy and the beveled looking glass in the corner.
Clearly her host was not accustomed to visitors or
servants.

Not feeling up to snuff, she snuggled back down
into the warmth of the blankets. She would wait to
see who came to her, for she did not see her gown
anywhere. As she lay there trying to come to grips
with her situation, her mind returned to the question of why? Why had Barlow thrown her into the
river?

The old servant was a frightful sight, but she'd
always had the impression he was rather a benign

entity who quietly did his mistress's bidding. She sat up once again as the shock of truth dawned. Barlow did as he was told. Which could only mean that her stepmother had ordered him to get rid of her. Lady Whitefield wanted her dead.

Dead! A new chill raced through her that had nothing to do with her health. Or was she merely being fanciful? Had it been an accident?

Sarah lay back against the pillows. She wasn't certain of what had truly happened on that bridge, but until she knew she couldn't return home. It might not be safe. Was it all about Aunt Phoebe's legacy? The fortune that she could not touch for years would likely go to Lucinda at Sarah's death. There was no proof of what she suspected, but her stepmother was single-minded if nothing else, and sooner or later she or her servant would succeed in getting rid of Sarah, permanently, if that was her intention.

What was she to do? Her first thought was to go to Ella or Lady Rose, but without funds that was out of the question for they both lived in distant counties. Besides, there was little likelihood that either girl's family would take her in, considering their disinterest in their own relatives. The truth was, without so much as a farthing in her pockets, she was stranded here, wherever here might be. Her only solution would be to write the solicitor. She was certain that if she explained and asked him to send her funds, he would gladly help her as he'd offered.

The light from the windows eventually faded, leaving the room in deep shadows. Night was once again falling. Sarah's eyes grew heavy and her last thought was that her host could certainly use a maid. Perhaps she could apply for a position and remain here while she waited for Mr. Cornell to help.

* * *

"Is she awake yet?" Jamie asked his brother the first thing the morning after they'd retrieved the mysterious lady from the river. The others crowded round, having just finished their breakfast.

Ronald shook his head. "Not when Peter and I visited her earlier. Shall we go and see if Rowdy's crowing has done the trick? Mama always used to say the henhouse was too close to the cottage."

The seven boys trekked to their late mother's room, Percy, ever curious, followed behind and settled on the rug while the boys formed a semicircle round the bed of the still-sleeping woman. She looked much better than when they had discovered her near the river. The mud had been wiped from her face and her cheeks held a rosy glow.

Peter tapped Jamie's shoulder and leaned over to whisper, "I say, have you noticed how much our river lady looks like Mama? With her hair dry and curling on the pillow, it was like when we used to visit Mama in the morning before she . . ." The lad looked down at his hands, unable to finish the painful sentence.

About to shake his head at his brother's usual fanciful ideas, Jamie paused staring pointedly at the lady's face. While their guest was years younger than their mother, she did look very much like Cassandra Ward had before the loss of their father and before her failing health had ravaged her appearance of raven black hair, pale ivory skin, and lovely features. There were differences, for the lady's mouth was fuller than his mother's and her nose a bit straighter, but at a glance one very well might mistake the women. If only it were Mama sleeping there—he pushed the thoughts of his mother aside before his eyes welled with tears. There were things to see to; he hadn't time to be weeping. "She is very pretty. I wonder who she is. But then it shan't matter in the end. No doubt our guest will return home as soon as she is able and we shall never see her again."

Ronald moved to the bed to touch her forehead and see if her fever had broken. He gently lay the back of his hand upon her brow, but before he could announce the results, the lady's eyes flew open, causing him to step back with a start. She sat up clutching the blankets to her, looking about the room, her eyes dazed. She blinked twice as if to clear her vision. Her head moved from left to right, surveying the many faces staring at her, then a smile tipped her full mouth, nearly making the boys gasp at her beauty.

"Good morning." Her voice was melodic, but slightly husky.

Jamie stepped forward. "Good morning, miss. How are you feeling?"

She brushed a dark tangled curl back from her ivory cheek. "A bit shaky, but I think all I have suffered for my soaking is a cold. Where am I?"

"You are at Wild Rose Cottage just a few miles east of Shrewsbury."

"Shrewsbury! Why that is half a county away from . . ." The lady fell silent, but the rigid set of her shoulders seemed to relax a bit. Her gaze once again swept the seven faces watching her curiously, as if she didn't know what to say.

Remembering his manners, Jamie gave a slight bow. "I am Jamie Ward and these are my brothers." He quickly ran through the names and each sketched a bow, as they had seen their eldest brother do. "And that is Percy." He pointed at the hairy dog who had settled on the rug in front of the unlit fireplace. "We found you unconscious by the river yesterday and brought you here."

"I am very pleased to meet you all. Pray, would one of you summon your mother? I must thank her for her hospitality and beg a favor of her."

Trepidation filled Jamie. He'd been afraid of this from the moment they'd found her at the river's edge. "Our mother died some months ago." He paused only a moment, then changed the subject. "If you should like to write a letter to someone to tell them of your circumstances, I can take it to town and post if for you."

"No, no, that isn't what I want. There is no one I must notify at present." She nibbled at her lip for a moment, her blue eyes grew thoughtful, then she smiled at the boys. "Who is taking care of you?"

Jamie exchanged a look with Ronald, then shrugged. There was simply no way they could keep this a secret from their guest. "Our father was lost at sea over a year ago, and Mama took quite ill. That's when we came here to live. Then she, too, was gone and we were left in the charge of Phillips, my late father's groom. He disappeared three weeks ago while on a trip to Shrewsbury, but we are certain he shall return any day now."

The young lady's eyes widened. "Do you mean the seven of you are living here alone, without anyone to take care of you?"

Jamie shifted uncomfortably. "We have managed, Miss, er, what is your name?"

"Miss Sarah Whiting," came the reply, but the lady seemed distracted, as if what she'd just learned had left her full of doubts.

Determined to make her understand, Jamie said, "Miss Whiting, I am twelve and quite capable of taking care of my brothers. Why, there are young boys my age who are already in the King's Army and working on naval ships. There is no need to inform anyone of my mother's passing. Besides, I am certain Phillips shall return any day. He is very loyal."

She placed a comforting hand on his shoulder. "I am certain that he is. Have you no relative who could come and stay? I do not mean to imply that this servant is not worthy, but surely—"

"There is no one, miss. We are quite alone, but we shall manage for we have money to buy what we need." His chin came up and he glared defiantly as the others behind him murmured agreement.

Sarah's gaze fell to her hands as she nervously began to play with the coverlet. "Then perhaps I might stay awhile and help you take care of the others until I inform my solicitor of my whereabouts and he can send me funds, for I . . . I have nowhere to go and lost everything when I was swept away by the flood."

"Have you no family either?" Peter asked from the end of the bed.

She sadly shook her head. "No blood relative, and I would prefer that no one know I am here."

Jamie's brow rose at the thought that the lady might have secrets as well, then an idea suddenly struck him. "Ronnie, take the boys into the parlor. I should like to have a word with Miss Whiting."

Ronald looked questioningly at his brother but did as he was bidden. When the door closed, Jamie stared intently at the lady. "We would be delighted for you to stay with us, miss. But I should like to ask a favor of you."

Sarah smiled. "I owe you my life, young sir. What can I do?"

He moved to the end of the bed as if he needed a moment to gather his thoughts. Sarah was struck with how adult he acted for his age, but then life had a way of stripping away one's childhood with harsh reality. At last he spoke, even as he plucked nervously at the buttons on his green vest. "Peter remarked on how much you look like our mother."

"Do I? I can assure you we are not related, for I would know if I had such delightful young relatives." She smiled at him, wondering what had made him suddenly so uneasy.

"Oh, I know that. Mama was an orphan after her parents died of the ague before she married Papa." He hesitated a moment, before he said, "I—I want you to pretend to be our mother." Seeing the shock on her face, he rushed to add, "Just for a while. Pray, let me explain." He went and retrieved a straight-backed chair and placed it beside the bed.

She watched and waited in silence, incredulous but still intrigued by what he proposed.

"This cottage belongs to the Earl of Longmire. As Mama explained it to me, the old earl intended us to live here rent-free for all of Mama's lifetime. Just before she died she summoned me and Phillips and made us swear not to tell a soul of her death. We were to bury her quietly and merely pretend she was still here, still ailing and unable to see visitors. Do you see the problem?"

Sarah nodded. "You think you will be sent away should the earl learn of your mother's death. But if he cared enough for your mother to give her a home, surely he will want her children to continue to be sheltered here."

Jamie shook his head. "I know nothing of that, for I never met the gentleman save his one visit after Papa died, but it doesn't matter, for the old earl is dead. He and one of his sons were killed in an accident soon after Mama was buried, and now the new earl is wanting to meet with Mama to discuss the cottage."

Sarah's brows drew together. "Did the gentleman say why? Surely, he cannot override the old earl's wishes if they were drawn up legally."

"Phillips thinks the son wants us out of here for this is a very valuable property, the best on the estate. He put his lordship off, saying Mama wasn't up to visitors. It worked for a while, but I think the gentleman is growing impatient. Since Philly's disappeared, we've only just managed to keep away from the new earl."

It suddenly occurred to Sarah that the servant's disappearance might not be a case of desertion due to a fondness for gin as is often the case with the lower orders. How badly did this earl want his cottage back? She shuddered when she realized how easy it would be to make seven small boys disappear as well. Then she realized her experience on the bridge was causing her to be fanciful. There was likely a reasonable explanation for everything, including the earl wanting to speak with Mrs. Ward. All she knew for certain was that she could not abandon these children, no matter their assertion that they could manage on their own.

Sarah patted the boy's hand, which clutched at her blanket in distress. "I will gladly stay and help you, but I don't see any need to impersonate Mrs. Ward. Perhaps if I explained matters to the new earl."

Jamie's slumped back into the chair. "It won't be enough that there is someone to take care of us. Philly says the law would be on his side. He'll send us to the workhouse if he learns the truth about Mama's death. We need you to convince him that Mama lives, then he will go away."

Her heart ached for the boys and all they had

lost, but she knew it would be foolish to undertake such a risky affair as to pretend to be their mother. Still, she didn't have the heart to tell him no at the moment. There had to be some other way. Then she remembered Mr. Cornell. He would be able to tell her what they should do. She thought it best not to tell Jamie just yet. It might be some time before the solicitor could come.

"I shall give the idea some serious consideration since it is so important. For the present do you think I might have some tea and toast? Shall I rise and make it myself? Where is my gown?"

He stood up, a smile lighting his face. "You stay in bed, and I shall go at once and bring you your breakfast. We don't want your cold becoming worse. Your gown was quite muddy and I put it in the wash-tub to soak. When you are feeling better you can wear Mama's dresses for you are much the same size." He walked to a tall oak wardrobe and threw open the door, exposing many colorful gowns. "Oh, you're a great gun, Miss Whiting."

The boy hurried from the room before Sarah could remind him she would only consider doing what he had asked. She settled back into the covers, thinking about their situation. The boys' discovery of her had been fortuitous. She could help them and would have a safe haven from her stepmother until she could contact Mr. Cornell. Her gaze swept the room. She realized she would need all her strength if the rest of the cottage's condition was anything like this room. Jamie thought he needed her to pretend to be their mother, but in truth, they needed a real mother.

Three

That same afternoon a visitor rapped sharply on the door of the cottage. In the rear parlor, Jamie shot a worried glance at Ronald, who halted mid-sentence in a story he was reading to Luther and Mark. The other boys, playing with a dissected map on the floor, sat up and looked warily at their eldest brother, but remained silent. Standing, Jamie said, "Perhaps if we are quiet they will go away."

Ronald peered in the direction of the front hall. The knocking became more insistent. "I fear not. Someone is quite determined."

Putting a finger over his lips as a signal for the younger ones to be quiet, Jamie left the parlor, closing the door behind him. His mind raced as he walked into the foyer with lagging steps. Very likely it was Lord Longmire, or worse, Mr. Joiner, who managed the estate for the earl. Would it be possible to once again turn the visitor away?

With a trembling hand, Jamie cracked the door only wide enough to look out and discover the ruddy-faced steward of Longdale. The boy swallowed the great lump that formed in his throat, and announced in a voice that squeaked a bit, "My mother is still quite ill and cannot be disturbed."

Joiner put his hand on the door and gave it a

slight shove, forcing it open and causing Jamie to fall back. "I'm not leaving here till I speak with Mrs. Ward, boy. That's all there is to it. I'll not be bamboozled again."

Jamie's knees shook. What was he to do? Would Miss Whiting help them by pretending to be their mother? But the lady was asleep, and he had no time to again plead with her to play the role. Perhaps if he merely showed the man their guest that would be enough to satisfy him. The steward would be convinced that their mother was there and all was well at the cottage. "Very well, sir, come this way. Please be quiet. The doctor does not want her rest disturbed."

In one of his mother's lawn night rails and a frilly nightcap, Sarah lay in a light doze. Unaware of the arrival of Mr. Joiner until the door to the bedchamber swung open, she awoke to Jamie's low whisper. "There you see her, sir. Do not—"

Basil Joiner, unwilling to return to his master thwarted again, pushed past the boy and walked straight into the bedchamber where his prey lay. Pulling the slouch hat from his head, exposing a pate bristled with gray stubble, he said, "Good morning, ma'am. I been wantin' to speak with ye for some time."

Fear drained all the color from Sarah's face, inadvertently helping her to look the part of the ailing Mrs. Ward. Her first panic-filled thought was that her stepmother had sent the burly man to find her. "S—sir, what do you want?"

"My apologies for bargin' in, ma'am, but his lordship's is wantin' to have a word with ye about the cottage."

Relieved that there was no immediate danger to her person, Sarah looked to Jamie, whose eyes were wide with fear and pleading. She realized at once that this was one of the men the lad feared would discover that Mrs. Ward was dead. There was no time to debate the right or wrong of what he'd asked her to do. She could not fail him. Taking the plunge, she folded her hands on the blanket and asked, "What is the matter . . . er"—she suddenly realized she didn't know the man's name—"sir?"

"The new earl has some things he wants to discuss, ma'am."

Joiner stared at her so pointedly Sarah knew a sudden urge to confess, but she was determined to help the boys. The one thing she didn't want was Lord Longmire coming to see her. He might take it in his head to throw her in the gaol if he discovered the truth, or worse, return her to her stepmother, whose intent might be deadly. "I—I am not well, sir. I cannot imagine what the gentleman could have to say to me. Is there some problem?"

"His lordship wishes to discuss the terms of your tenancy, Mrs. Ward."

She couldn't risk meeting with Longmire. He might well be acquainted with the late widow and then all would be ruined. "S—sir, I cannot have visitors as yet. Pray inform his lordship, when I am better I shall send word. All is as it should be here and we have no wish to vary the terms that his lordship's father established. I must not be disturbed."

The man's dark eyes grew to tiny slits. "When does Wimple come again?"

Sarah froze. She didn't have the least notion whom he was talking about. "I—I that is—"

Jamie stepped forward. "The first Monday of the month, Mr. Joiner."

The steward's gaze roved curiously about the

room as the boy spoke. His brushy brows flattened into a disapproving line at the unkempt room. "Where is Phillips? I should like a word with him."

"Gone to visit his ailing father," Jamie replied readily, with the falsehood he'd used in Shrewsbury with all the merchants.

About to once again speak, Sarah interrupted the steward. "Mr. Joiner, I am greatly fatigued. Pray send my best wishes to the new earl and inform him that as soon as I am better I shall invite him to Wild Rose Cottage to take tea." She then closed her eyes and prayed that the man would take the hint.

Quick to take her lead, Jamie hurried to the door. "This way, sir."

Joiner, clearly not satisfied with the outcome of the interview gave a discontented grunt, then reluctantly departed. He didn't know what he would tell Lord Longmire, for he'd accomplished little with his brazen visit other than to at last meet the illusive Mrs. Ward. His face grew thoughtful. She was certainly more beautiful than he remembered. But then he'd scarcely seen the woman on her arrival. That morning she'd been bundled in a shawl, scarcely looking at her surroundings, with those cursed boys swarming round her like bees. Her present appearance explained a great deal about the old earl's fascination with the lady. Joiner reassured himself he'd done his best. With that, he mounted his horse and set out for Longdale Hall.

Back in the bedroom, Sarah sat up, shaking all over. There was a part of her that wanted to throttle Jamie for bringing the steward to her without her permission. Yet having met the stern man, she had to admire the lad for having the gumption to stand up to the fellow.

The door to her room opened and Jamie returned, a shaky grin on his young face as he nearly strutted to her bed. Despite his bravado, the encounter clearly had shaken him. His face was deadly pale and beads of moisture glistened on his brow. "You did a grand thing, Miss Whiting. You saved us. Fooled old Joiner completely."

"Jamie, can you not see how dangerous a thing this is you are asking me to do? I had no notion who Mr. Wimple was."

The lad settled on the chair near the bed, looking exhausted from the close call. With a dismissive sweep of his hand, he said, "Oh, him. That's a local workman who comes and does chores around the cottage such as fixing the shutters or trimming the roses—whatever is needed. He's not important for he has never spoken to Mama, only with Philly."

"Still, there are so many things I do not know about your life. Things that Lord Longmire may know. It would be a disaster for me to try and play your mother. I cannot—"

"But you already have done it and very successfully." Jamie sat forward and grasped her hand. "We truly need you. There is not likely to be another visitor here for months now that we have fobbed off the steward. Please don't say no, Miss Whiting."

Sarah would have to have a heart of stone to deny the look of entreaty in the young lad's eyes. Besides, the cottage could keep her safe as well. Very likely she was going to regret her decision, but she smiled at him. "Don't you think you should call me Mother since I am to stay, for one slip of the tongue could ruin us."

Jamie threw his arms around her neck. "I should be proud to call you Mama."

Tears welled up in Sarah's eyes. It felt good to be appreciated. In many ways she and the Ward brothers were a perfect match. She needed a family, and they needed someone to take care of them. All she could do was pray that Lord Longmire didn't learn the truth.

"Well, then, sit down and tell me everything you can about your life here at the cottage."

"What do you mean you cannot find her body?" Lady Whitefield shouted at Barlow. She stood up so suddenly from the cherrywood escritoire where she'd been writing, her chair fell backward. "I must know that she is dead before I go to Mr. Cornell."

The old servant shuffled forward and righted the chair before he answered his mistress. "I seen her go under the water, my lady. Certain I am that she's dead. Ye needn't worry yer head about that."

"Oh, Barlow, don't be a fool. I need more than your certainty. I need a body for the vicar. For the solicitor." The dowager began to pace back and forth, the black gown she'd donned for appearance's sake detracting not one whit from her beauty.

The old man scratched his head. "Well, if it's a body you be wantin' I can go to the graveyard at Montford and dig—"

Her face etched with horror, Lady Whitefield shrieked, "Don't you dare, you fool." The lady muttered for several moments about witless servants before she at last regained her composure. She spoke to Barlow with measured patience. "I don't want just *any* body. I want *Sarah's* body."

"Don't see why. It ain't like we can cart the thing to London to show that lawyer fellow. It would stink somethin' fierce 'afore we was out of the county, 'specially after bein' in the water for days. Likely we'd arrive in Town with a flock of carrion on the roof of the—"

"That will be enough of that." The lady shuddered, then her face grew thoughtful. "Maybe if I take you to the solicitor, and you tell him that you saw the wretched girl drown that will do the trick."

"I'll swear to it, my lady."

Lady Whitefield's gaze moved to the document she'd been forging with such diligence. It was worth a try. "Have the carriage ready first thing in the morning. We are for London."

After the groom left, her ladyship sat down and reread what she'd written. All it needed was the final signature and two witnesses. She picked up one of the letters Sarah had sent home from school and with surprising skill duplicated the signature at the bottom. Holding the will up, Lucinda decided that it would pass inspection by Mr. Cornell.

She put the document down, then picked up the quill. While she pondered what names to use as her witnesses, she tapped the feather against her chin. Careful to vary the signatures, she signed Cook's name, for Lucinda knew the woman wouldn't risk her job by denying she had signed in Sarah's presence.

The second one proved more difficult. The dowager knew it must be someone who would either lie for her or else someone the solicitor wouldn't be able to question. It suddenly came to her that her friend, Amelia Baker's son, had just left for Boston. What was his name? Abel, Abbot, Abner that was it. With a bold flourish, she penned Abner Baker as her final witness. Finished, she admired her handiwork before folding the document and putting it into a small leather pouch.

The task done, she rose and went to the looking

glass that hung over the mantelpiece. Despite her
extreme distress at the news Barlow had carried,
there was not a golden curl out of place. A smile
parted lips that were enhanced to red with a bit of
rouge. "By this time next week, you shall be the
wealthy and beautiful Lady Whitefield, newest Toast
of London."

Sarah awoke the following morning and donned
one of Cassandra Ward's dresses, a blue-sprigged
muslin that barely fit. With a final tug at the low-cut
bodice of the gown, she was ready to begin her new
duties as mother to seven boys. That is, until she
stepped from the bedroom where she'd been
lodged and took her first look at the inside of Wild
Rose Cottage. As she roved through the lower rooms
she found dust, clutter, and mud in abundance, not
to mention toys, books, and discarded garments
tossed about at will. Three weeks with their servant
gone showed that seven boys without the least clue
about housekeeping had taken its toll on the cottage.

The kitchen proved even worse than the parlors.
Dirty pots, pans, glasses, and dishes cluttered every
surface in the room. The slate floor seemed as if it
hadn't seen a mop or broom in months, as large
dark blots of debris flecked the gray surface. The
room looked a daunting task, but she pushed up
her sleeves, found a clean apron in a drawer, and
set about putting everything in order. She lit a fire
in the stove, which fitted into the wall beside the
open fireplace. While the wood crackled loudly, she
filled the stove's boiler to heat water for washing the
dishes. That done, she swept the floor.

The boys would soon be awake, so she inspected

the larder, hoping to prepare something special for them for their first breakfast together. It seemed that Jamie's one skill had been to boil eggs, of which the boys had soon tired.

The small pantry was surprisingly well stocked, so she cleared the surface of one of the kitchen tables and began to prepare scones. By the time the small currant-filled rolls were ready for the oven, the water in the boiler was hot, so she set the little breads to bake and began washing up the piles of dirty crockery.

Some thirty minutes later, the door to the kitchen opened and Jamie entered. He halted and looked around. "Why, Miss Whiting, you have performed a miracle. It looks just like when Philly was here."

Putting down a drying towel, she put her arms akimbo. "I want it to remain this way from now on, young man. When dirty dishes are returned to the kitchen, into the wash pan they go."

Jamie grinned. "You sound just like Mama after she and Philly returned from her first meeting with Lord Longmire."

Before Sarah could comment, the door again opened and the other boys trouped into the kitchen. Ronald sniffed the air. "What is that wonderful smell?"

"Scones, but you shall have to earn them." Sarah moved to the stove to remove the golden brown rolls.

"Earn them?" Adam said, "I don't see why—"

Alan piped, "What would you have us do . . . Mother?"

Sarah's gaze flew to the sweet-tempered twin and she saw that he and the others, save Adam and the very bashful Luther, were smiling. It seemed they were adjusted to the idea that she must be addressed as their parent for safety's sake.

She slid the piping hot tray of rolls onto the table, then laid out her bargain. "Today shall be wash day. I want all your dirty clothes and the linens from your beds down by the washtub in the next quarter hour. By then I should have your breakfast on the table and waiting. After we eat we shall clean the parlors."

She didn't have to ask a second time. The boys rushed from the kitchen and within moments the sounds of footsteps clattered on the stairs. About to remove the scones from the pan, she paused when she realized Luther, who'd never spoken a word to her, still lingered at the door. She moved to kneel in front of him. "Is something wrong, Luther?"

He shook his head. There was a long pause before he mustered the courage to say, "I'm glad you are staying, miss." With that he rushed from the room. Sarah's throat grew tight as she batted back tears. She was rapidly falling in love with her new "sons." There could be no denying this was going to be a great deal of work, but she was glad she was staying.

Moving back to the table to finish preparing their breakfast, her thoughts dwelled on the boys. There wasn't just the matter that they needed someone to cook and clean for them. They might well need someone to protect them from the earl, who seemed to have designs on their cottage. She would do her best to see them safe and comfortable in their home.

A week later a pair of gray Arabians cantered along at a steady but sedate pace down the road from Shrewsbury, two men on their backs. The gentleman riding in the lead, handling his reins rather stiffly, bore little resemblance to the one in the Beaumont library more than a week earlier. His unruly auburn locks had been trimmed into a neat Brutus style, the red stubble shaven from his face. Ten days of sunshine had replaced his pallor with a light bronze tint and his improved diet was well on the way to removing the hollows in his cheeks.

Well turned out in a black beaver hat, blue riding coat, over a gray waistcoat and buckskins ending with well polished Hessians, Sir Evan looked the epitome of the young gentleman of fashion. Riding just to the left of the baronet was Hawks, ever alert to signs of fatigue in the former officer, but the trip would be a short one, for they had departed the wedding breakfast at the Hall just after the bride and groom. After finding rooms at a Shrewsbury Inn, the baronet and the earl, having determined that there should be no connection known about them in the neighborhood, Sir Evan set out to meet the questionable Mrs. Cassandra Ward.

"I believe the cottage is just round this corner, Hawks. We shall see what the new Lady Longmire is so determined about."

The servant made a rude sound in his throat. "It just don't seem right to me to be takin' a family's cottage on the whims of some flighty female, sir." Hawks had briefly met the earl's new bride after the wedding. The valet found her quite pretty but excessively silly and even a bit spoiled. But perhaps he was being unfair since it was her wedding day and more likely it was the nerves of a young maiden facing the mysteries of her wedding night that had made her appear so.

The servant's words echoed in Sir Evan's mind.

That worrisome thought had consumed him since he'd arrived in Shropshire. Mrs. Fleming and her daughters were perfectly respectable people, but he wondered how much time they would truly spend in the country, with two younger sisters to present. Somehow it didn't seem right to uproot a family of seven children from their home just so Lady Longmire could have her mama and sisters nearby a few months of the year.

Still, as Titus had reminded him, there was some question about Mrs. Ward's respectability and in what manner she'd finagled her way into the cottage. One didn't want one's wife having to daily face the possibility of meeting the likes of a stage actress on the grounds of one's estate. It simply wasn't the thing.

Rounding the curve, the men reined their horses to a walk as the cottage came into view. The place was larger than Sir Evan had expected. The morning sun glistened on the dew-laden leaves of the rosebushes, giving the thatched cottage a magical quality as if in some dream. The front windows were open and the muted sounds of a pianoforte, well played, drifted on the breeze as well as the pleasing aroma of cinnamon. He knew in an instant what it was about the cottage that had enchanted Lady Longmire. The place was like a sanctuary from all that was dark and grim in the world. Here nestled in the quiet woods, one could believe that nothing bad could ever happen.

The servant interrupted Sir Evan's musings. "What's the plan for meetin' this elusive female, sir?"

"At the moment, I haven't a clue, Hawks. I am open to suggestions."

Before either man could make another comment,

a great hairy brown-and-white dog came bounding from behind the cottage, barking at the strangers who'd invaded his domain. There was nothing vicious about the animal, only a pet's protective instincts for what his boundaries were.

"Leave things to me, sir," Hawks announced, smiling as he watched the animal. Suddenly he veered the gray he rode to the stone fence. With the skill of a traveling circus performer, the valet made the horse rear on its haunches in front of the barking dog. The Arabian whinnied his protest at such treatment, causing even the dog to stop his yapping for a moment and sidle away from the spirited steed.

To Sir Evan's utter amazement, Hawks hurled himself off the horse over the fence into the garden of Wild Rose Cottage. He landed on the other side of the stone wall with a soft thump and began to moan like the wind during a gale at sea. Uncertain if his servant had inadvertently injured himself during his performance, the baronet jumped from his horse. He grabbed the reins of the second animal and tied them both to the gatepost, then leaned over the wall.

He discovered the man writhing on the ground. "Are you unharmed?"

Hawks ceased his performance for a moment and winked. "Right as rain, sir." With that he let out another wrenching moan and clutched at his ankle.

The front door to the cottage opened slowly, then a small army of dark-haired young lads poured into the garden. Sir Evan knew little of children, but from his nieces and nephews he could tell there was a goodly range of ages, starting from near four or five years going up to early teens. With his gaze riveted on the open portal, he nearly gasped when the most beautiful raven-haired woman he'd ever set eyes upon appeared in the opening. She hesitated but a moment, taking in the man prostrate in her garden.

Upon realizing what had happened, the lady hurried down the front walk to where Hawks lay, giving the baronet a chance to take a closer look at her. She was a Diamond of the First Water. A yellow-and-white stripped gown clung to her lithe figure as she dashed down the flagstone walk. Her black hair hung in loose curls to her waist, held back by a yellow ribbon. A heart-shaped face displayed deep blue eyes, a straight nose above temptingly full lips that were pursed with concern as she stooped to help Hawks.

"How are you injured, sir?" Her voice held a musical lilt that made Sir Evan long to hear more. In a word the lady was utterly enchanting.

Hawks moaned and held his booted foot.

Sir Evan forced himself to stop his ogling and to remember his mission. He stepped into his role, knowing what Hawks intended. "It appears he has injured his ankle, Miss . . ."

The lady looked up at him. Her blue eyes widened a moment at the sight of him. He attributed the startled look to the scars that stood out on his face and resisted the urge to turn to one side.

She stammered, "Er, Miss—"

One of the larger boys stepped forward and interrupted, "She is our mama, Mrs. Ward, sir." He eyed the gentlemen warily.

"Sir Evan Beaumont, ma'am, and this is my valet, Hawks. We were riding down the road when your dog frightened one of the horses, and I fear my man was tossed to the ground." A twinge of conscience tugged at him for the May game they were playing, but he knew of no other way to gain entry into the lady's life.

She stood up, and distractedly began to smooth down her skirt and the apron she wore. Mesmerized, Sir Evan's gaze followed the motion of her hands as they had moved up to just below her bodice. He noted that her shapely breast nearly spilled from the top of the gown, almost as if the garment weren't cut for her. Yet he didn't complain, for it was a pleasant sight that stirred his masculinity.

Realizing where his thoughts were heading, he tamped down the unexpected lusty urge. This was a woman who very likely used her physical assets to get what she wanted if what Titus suspected was true. There could be no denying she was lovely enough to be on the stage. An actress who had been very busy off stage, he thought as his gaze swept over the small faces watching him. When he returned his gaze to the mother, he was struck with how youthful she appeared. But then he'd heard such women had artifices to make themselves look younger.

The lady interrupted his wandering thoughts. "You and your servant must come inside, sir. We must see to his ankle. Hopefully it is only sprained. Jamie, Ronald, help Mr. Hawks. Peter, open the gate for Sir Evan."

The gentleman stood a moment, watching the older boys assist his servant up the walk behind Mrs. Ward, who'd hurried ahead to open the door. The younger boys, he realized, were all watching him as if he were the tooth-drawer come to ply his trade on each and everyone. He mustered his most charming smile and asked, "Is there somewhere I might put my horses? Don't want them standing out here on the road."

One boy, a mirror image of the one beside him, stepped forward. He was a sleepy-eyed lad but owned obvious pluck. "I'm Alan, sir, and this is Adam. We'll take them to the small shed out back."

His twin puckered up. "I don't see why—"

The first boy elbowed his brother. "Hush and come on."

The two boys scaled the fence and took the horses, leading them to the end of the stone wall, then disappeared behind the cottage. Peter stood holding the gate, while the two smaller ones stayed to one side watching the stranger. Sir Evan smiled at the two little boys, but one dashed and hid behind his brother at the gate, the other one sneezed.

"I've a cold, sir," the little one announced and returned a bold stare. Then he rubbed his nose on his sleeve.

Amused, Sir Evan said, "Then we'd best take you back inside, my good fellow." He stepped through the gate and started up the walk. The boy called Peter hurried up beside him, peering at him with obvious interest.

"Are you a soldier, sir? Is that how you got those scars?"

The baronet's hand moved involuntarily to the cursed scars he thought disfigured his face. "I was." He looked down at the boy, who watched him with eager interest, but no revulsion. His hand dropped away as he realized what Hawks had said was true. One should be proud of the scars one earned defending one's country. "I was injured at Toulouse and had to sell out my commission. Should you like to be a soldier?"

The lad shook his head. "I will be a sailor like my father, and captain ships to all the distant ports. I intend to capture a mermaid and bring her back to England to prove to everyone that they do exist.

Jamie and Ronald only laugh when I tell then that, but I'll show them."

Listening to the mixture of truth and wild imagining, Sir Evan was struck with an idea. He halted, then smiled. "So, your father was a sailor. What did your mother do while he was away at sea?"

The boy opened his mouth, then he froze before uttering a word. His blue eyes narrowed and a shuttered look came into his face. "We are not to discuss our mother with strangers, sir. Follow me and I shall take you to the parlor."

There could be little doubt Titus was correct. There was some secret here at the cottage, but only time would tell what the truth was. With a last look around, Sir Evan followed the boy into the cottage.

He was led to a parlor at the back of the cottage. It was a pleasant room that opened on to a rear garden that was as wild and magical as the front of the cottage. Near the unlit fireplace he found Hawks, his foot on an ottoman, playing his part to the hilt.

"Do be careful, ma'am," the servant said, holding off Mrs. Ward and one of the older boys from removing his boot. "I think it's just a sprain. If I could rest here just for a time, I'm certain I shall be able to continue our trip."

To the baronet's surprise the young boy, who stood after running his hands over the booted ankle, announced, "It doesn't appear to be broken." He then noted the quizzical look on Sir Evan's face and fell silent.

The lady patted the boy's back. "Ronald wants to be a doctor. We always find his judgment to be sound." With that the boy moved to stand beside the others. A moment of awkward silence settled on the room, then the boys' mother stared thoughtfully at Sir Evan. "You might want to send for a physician once you return home, sir."

Determined not to be enchanted by her beauty, he smiled and nodded, looking at the small models of sailing ships on the mantelpiece. "That I shall, ma'am. We are staying in town at the Mellow Monk, but I am looking for a house to let in the country. Do you know of any?"

A sudden silence filled the room, causing him to look back at her. He discovered she was staring at the boy who'd spoken in the yard, a dismayed expression on her face. "I . . . that is—"

The lad interrupted, "There's nothing this side of Shrewsbury save Lord Longmire's properties and I don't think he has anything available for lease."

The lady's cheeks grew pink, then she stuttered, "I—I am not as well acquainted with such matters as my son." Squaring her shoulders, she asked, "Would you care for some refreshments while Mr. Hawks rests, sir?"

"That would be most welcome, Mrs. Ward."

A look of relief flooded her face. "I shall see to it." With that she exited the room.

Seven hostile stares bored into him as he stood beside Hawks. He couldn't have been more uncomfortable had he stumbled into a French encampment during the war. Searching for something to say, the baronet asked, "Might I know your names?"

"I am Jamie, sir." With that the boy quickly ran through the names of the others. The future physician was introduced as Ronald, the mermaid fancier was Peter, the grouchy twin answered to Adam while the sleepy-eyed one was called Alan. The two youngest were introduced as Luther, who still hid behind his elder brother Jamie, then came little Mark, who offered up a new sneeze as he grinned at Sir Evan.

The gentleman stood clutching his hat and gloves, wondering if the family gave everyone the silent treatment or just him. But he was determined to help Titus, which meant breaking through the Wards' barriers. "Such a wonderful smell coming from the kitchen."

Peter announced, "Mother made us cinnamon buns today. She cooks something special every morning."

Hawks looked up at Sir Evan, a question in his gaze. They both knew Ladies of Quality rarely cooked. "Your mother bakes? Have you no cook?"

Jamie glared at his brother, clearly upset by the boy's loose tongue. "Our servant, Phillips, has gone to visit his sick father. We are expecting his return any day now. Until then, we have been helping Mother with the work." There was pride in his voice.

Struck with a sudden inspiration, Sir Evan put his hat and gloves on a nearby table. "We soldiers are quite useful in the kitchen. I shall lend your mother a hand. Hawks, entertain the lads till Mrs. Ward and I return with the refreshments."

He started toward the door he'd seen Cassandra Ward depart through, but Jamie dashed in front of him, trying to bar his way. "That's not necessary, sir. Mother can handle—"

But Sir Evan brushed his protests aside, moving past the boy. He was determined to speak with the lady of the house, to penetrate the secrecy of Wild Rose Cottage. He easily found the kitchen, a white-washed room with two open windows where pies had been set to cool on the sills. Neat rows of blue dishes were displayed in a hutch against one wall, copper pots hung from hooks above the fireplace, where a kettle steamed. He was suddenly reminded of the inviting warmth of his mother's kitchens back at Beaumont. Very often as a boy he would find her conferring with Cook. She would see that he had a glass of milk and a slice of cake and send him to play. The thought even now made him want to smile.

Then he spied Mrs. Ward across the room, removing teacups and saucers from a cupboard. As she turned around, her blue eyes widened at the sight of him. Clearly there was something about him that terrified her, and he didn't think it was his scarred face.

"Is there something you require, Sir Evan?" Her hands fidgeted with the crockery she held.

"Not at all. I came to lend a hand when I heard that you were doing all the work alone." He moved to take the cups from her, following her to the table, where a wooden tray lay. "I was ten years a soldier, Mrs. Ward. One learns to be very self-sufficient, especially in regards to meals."

She hesitated only a moment, then with a glance at Jamie standing mutely at the door, she shrugged. "I shall not turn down any offers to help, sir. There is bread to be sliced as well as ham." She directed him to the door of the larder on the other side of the room.

Within minutes he was facing her across the large table with a knife, busily slicing the loaf of bread, managing as best he could with a hand that still didn't work quite properly. "It is most kind of you to invite us to tea."

Stacking cinnamon buns on a plate, she nodded as her gaze went to the scars on the back of his hand, but she made no mention of them. "I only hope Mr. Hawks will be back on his feet soon."

"He's a hardy fellow. I'm certain he will be walking again by this evening." Certain because he knew there was nothing wrong with the man.

The mother looked at young Jamie again, then with a strange nod of her head as if some secret communication had passed between them, she asked, "What brought you to Shropshire, Sir Evan?"

"A pair of testy grays and my old curricle." His green eyes twinkled at her as Jamie laughed.

Her lovely mouth twitched, before she said, "I mean what business have you here, sir? We are a good ways from London and not truly on the path to anywhere, save Wales."

"Actually, I'm simply on holiday. Six months at home in Dorsetshire, and that wander lust that affects most soldiers started to stir me once again. So I pulled out one of my late father's guidebooks and read about Shrewsbury and its ancient wall situated on the Severn and decided to ride up here and see it for myself. I've always had a passion for antiquities and I'm thinking of writing a book about the history of the town. Its churches are all quite famous."

There was some truth to what he said. Even as a boy he'd loved the study of ancient worlds and would love to write about some of the English battles he'd studied. He'd even taken the time to read about Shrewsbury and its illustrious Saxon history before setting out on his mission He stopped what he was doing, and asked, "Do you think this will be enough?"

Thick slices of bread were stacked on the plate in neat columns.

"Plenty." She smiled fully at him for the first time and his breath caught in his throat. He forced his mind back to what he was doing and set about slicing the ham while she poured boiling water into the large teapot.

"H—have you any friends in the neighborhood?" She looked up from what she was doing and there was almost a breathless anticipation as she awaited his answer.

"I am certain there must be someone in the county I know from my regiment, but I've no intention to call on anyone. After being at the army's beck and call for ten years, I've a mind to just wander where my whim takes me."

For the first time since he'd entered the cottage, Sir Evan felt a relaxing of the tension in both the woman and the child as smiles passed between them. Jamie stepped to the table and asked, "Were you with Wellington, sir? Did you fight at Salamanca or Talavera? Or experience the siege at Badajaz?"

Before the baronet could respond, Mrs. Ward said, "Don't pester Sir Evan about his war experiences, Jamie." Her gaze scanned the scars on his face and then his hands before she returned to pouring glasses of milk for the boys. "The subject may be painful."

"I don't mind talking about my experiences in the war."

"Then I'm certain the others would like to hear as well, for they all like a good story. Everything is ready, shall we go into the parlor?" She went to lift the tray.

"Let me." Sir Evan picked up the well-laden tray and followed the mother and son back into the parlor. His next thirty minutes were filled with a barrage of questions from the older boys as they all enjoyed their repast. He and his servant told amusing tales of life as soldiers in the Peninsula, leaving the darker side of war unspoken of in front of the young lads. Between the tales of adventuring in the Portuguese mountains, he made subtle inquiries about their life, but found most of his questions avoided or answered with monosyllabic responses and a strain would again fall on the group. He would once again have to turn the topic of conversation to other matters.

With teacups drained and plates of food empty, Hawks lowered his foot to the floor and tested it, as if it were truly injured. "Well, I'm feelin' more the thing."

Sir Evan suddenly felt a fraud after the enjoyable time they'd just spent with the Ward family and rose. "We should be on our way. I must thank you for your hospitality, and I hope that you and your fine sons will do me the honor of coming to Shrewsbury one night for dinner."

All the tension seemed to rush back into the room. Jamie's eyes widened and his chin jutted, but it was his mother who said, "I thank you but must decline. We do not go out much. My health has been rather delicate since we moved to Shropshire."

Everything about her put the falsehood to her statement. She possessed a well-curved, robust figure beneath the ill-fitting gown. Her blue eyes were clear, her cheeks rosy, and her full lips a deep pink. He could not imagine a woman who looked more healthy—or more enticing.

"Then I shall have to think of some other way to repay your kindness. Come, Hawks, let us go. You wait out front and I shall bring the animals round." Before she could protest, he strode from the room, out the front door, and round the cottage to retrieve their horses.

The men mounted, called their good-byes, and rode away from the watching Wards. They were scarcely a quarter mile from the cottage when

Hawks said, " 'Tis a grand family but something's very strange there, sir."

"You sensed it too."

"Aye, that I did. Can't put my finger on what it is, but there's certainly something not right. I've seen toy soldiers livelier than them lads."

Sir Evan knew exactly what his servant meant. Boys that age were generally full of conversation and spirit, but the children he'd just left were as repressed and silent as prisoners at Newgate. The only spark of animation he'd seen was when the elder boys questioned him about life in the army. There was definitely something out of the ordinary going on at the cottage. A vision of pale blue eyes and shining black hair flashed in his mind and he promised himself to get to the bottom of the matter. He straightened in the saddle. It had nothing to do with his attraction to Mrs. Ward. He'd made a promise to Titus that he intended to keep and that's all it was.

Four

Sarah poured hot water into the basin, then turned and smiled at the four youngest boys. They stood in night shirts and eyed her warily. It was her penchant for cleanliness they feared the most. Their bedchamber was proof enough of her zeal. There was not a toy in sight, all storybooks were neatly lined on the shelf of an old cabinet, and the linens on the seven narrow beds were newly washed for the second time since she'd arrived. She'd been encouraging them for the past week to wash properly, but like most lads, they'd scrubbed their faces and hands, determining that was sufficient. It seemed tonight was to be different.

"This morning I noted that one could grow potatoes in the dirt behind those ears." She waited and when all remained silent she added, "That will not do."

Luther stood in bashful silence as Mark rubbed his nose with a sleeve. "I got's a cold and it ain't good to be wet. Ronnie said so."

Sarah shook her head. "It will only be for a moment, then you will be safely dried and in your bed."

Alan yawned as he sidled toward his cot. "I'm too sleepy. I'll do it in the morning."

Adam complained, "No one can see behind our

ears." He tugged his shaggy black locks over his ears.

She picked up a small bar of soap and a washing cloth. "No excuses tonight. Shall I do the honors or do you prefer to help one another?"

The boys exchanged a defeated look, then with a grumpy groan Adam stepped forward and took the cloth. "Oh, very well, but if we all die from the ague, it shall be on your head."

Sarah laughed. "You needn't worry. It is a pleasant night and no one will catch cold from a good wash." She stepped back and the boys crowded round the basin, Adam taking charge but complaining throughout the entire process. Within some ten minutes, with a great deal of splashing and as much water on the floor as in the basin, all the boys were clean and inspected by their surrogate mother and tucked into bed. She bid them good night, then returned to the kitchen to empty what little liquid remained in the basin. She went to the parlor, where the three eldest awaited her—Ronald reading while Jamie played a game of Impatience. Peter lay on the rug in front of the cold fireplace, moving tin soldiers about in a mock game of war. She couldn't help noticing he now called his favorite soldier Sir Evan.

Jamie dropped the cards to the table and moved to where Sarah settled with a basket of socks that needed darning. "I wanted to speak with you about our visitor."

"Sir Evan?" Sarah's gaze remained on her busy hands, but her cheeks warmed. There could be no excuse for the way she'd behaved this afternoon. Every time she'd looked at him, her heart had pounded, and she'd been utterly useless in protecting the boys' interests. If Jamie hadn't intervened, she might have given them away by uttering her real name. She couldn't explain it, for the baronet was not classically handsome, but there was something about him that had triggered a response in her heart. Perhaps it was the inquiring green eyes that seemed to peer into her soul or the slight tilt of his sculpted mouth as he smiled gently at them, but whatever it was she'd behaved foolishly and that must not happen again.

"Did you not think he asked far too many questions?" Jamie asked, watching her distractedly.

"No more so than any other stranger one first meets." She plied her needle, thinking about the gentleman's questions concerning Mrs. Ward's husband and their life before Wild Rose Cottage. They had seemed casual enough, and he hadn't pressed them for answers that hadn't been forthcoming.

"We've not had many visitors through the years, but Mama used to tell us never to be pert by asking questions that were none of our affair. That was just what Sir Evan did."

Her hands ceased their work and her pale blue gaze captured his deep blue one. "What are you suggesting, Jamie?"

"Might the gentleman be here for some reason other than to look at old churches? Philly once said that the earl's son, the one that just inherited, was rumored to be in the military." The boy's voice was low as if he didn't want his brothers to hear his suspicions.

Putting her needle down, she squeezed Jamie's hand. "I think your imagination is running wild. The gentleman comes from the south of England, Dorsetshire, I believe he said. He would have been in an entirely different regiment than your Lord Longmire because units are mostly mustered within the boundaries of a county. While they might have encountered one another, I cannot envision they would have been fast friends."

Jamie slumped back in his seat, a surprising frown on his normally smiling face. "I don't think we should see him anymore."

Sarah laughed. " 'Tis unlikely he will invite us to dine again. He was merely being polite and we have refused him. That is that." She couldn't deny that if things were different she would very much like to dine with the baronet, but the boys needed her and she must put aside fanciful thoughts of courting and romance for the present.

"I may only be twelve, Sarah, but I know that look in a gentleman's eyes. It was the same as Papa often gave Mama. Sir Evan is definitely interested in you in that way." A surprisingly knowing look settled into Jamie's eyes.

Startled by his intuitive grasp of the undercurrents of adult attraction, she dismissed his worries, thinking him a bit protective, or perhaps he was fearful she might fall in love and leave them. Ruffling his hair, she grinned. "Well, you needn't worry. I have seven men in my life already and that should be sufficient for any woman."

Peter, without looking up or showing he'd been listening in any way, announced, "Well, someone should have told Salty Sally who worked at the White Gull that, for she had ten different men every day of the week."

Sarah's cheeks warmed as she took the meaning of Sally's profession, but Jamie took his brother's comment in stride. His lips tilted upward as he winked at Sarah. "Just so, she was a bit greedy, was she not?"

The clock on the mantelpiece chimed the hour of nine, relieving her of having to comment about some unknown bawd from the boys' former life. Instead she arched one dark brow at the young man beside her and pointed at the timepiece.

"I know, I know," Jamie said, standing. "To bed we must go. Come, brothers. 'Tis time for us to retire."

They each kissed Sarah good night and bustled upstairs, Ronnie and Peter arguing over who might have the bed nearest the window that night. Percy trailed behind, hoping to find a spot on one of the smaller boys' beds. The rear parlor grew quiet and she returned to her mending, her thoughts drifting back to her conversation with Jamie. Was Sir Evan interested in her the way a man is with a woman? Her fingers trembled at the thought and she nearly missed a stitch. There was no denying that she found him attractive and wished with all her being that she might know him better. But she couldn't risk revealing the truth to a man she barely knew. She wouldn't endanger the boys' life at Wild Rose. There was also the matter of needing to keep hidden from her stepmother.

"Oh, if only Lucinda would go back to her family in Dorchester and leave me alone." Her voice echoed in the empty room.

Suddenly she sat up, horror etching her face. She tossed the darning back into the basket and went in search of the atlas the boys had used in the simple class she'd run that morning. Hands trembling, she thumbed through the book until she found the page she wanted. Dorsetshire County. The name of Dorchester seemed to leap off the page at her. Lucinda and Sir Evan were from the same county.

She slammed the book closed and pushed it away from her. Now who was letting her imagination run wild? But once the seed of worry had been planted, she couldn't let it go. Was there some connection between her stepmother and their visitor? Was her aunt so determined to get her inheritance that she would send someone to look for her?

"Good heavens, I am being utterly foolish." There were thousands of people in Dorsetshire. Lucinda couldn't know them all. Still, Sarah knew she mustn't discount her stepmother's determination. If the dowager had sent the baronet after her, she would have to be careful. He might be suspicious but he couldn't know for sure that she wasn't Cassandra Ward. After all, there had been no portraits of Sarah since she was twelve, when Father had commissioned one small miniature which, no doubt, Lucinda had discarded just as she had Sarah in sending her away to school. Sir Evan couldn't know what she looked like other than a description and, from what the boys said, Mrs. Ward had the same features as Sarah, black hair and blue eyes. Still, were she around the gentleman too much, she might slip up like she nearly had this afternoon. Jamie was right; they should avoid Sir Evan henceforth.

With a sad sigh, Sarah rose. Looking about the empty room, she felt completely alone, battling the world for the sake of the boys. Then it came to her she wasn't alone; there was the solicitor who'd been so kind. She'd been so overwhelmed with the duties at the cottage she'd failed to write Mr. Cornell. She went to a small writing desk and sat down, drawing out a sheet. What to tell him? Her life had gotten too complicated to put everything down in a letter. She would merely inform him where she was and tell him she desperately needed his help. She dipped the pen in ink and wrote in a neat, even style. Finished, she scrawled her name, then as a postscript, she requested that he keep her location a secret. She folded the missive and put the solicitor's direction on the front, then propped it on the desk. She would have to take it to Shrewsbury to post.

That done, she put out the candles save one, and retired to her room. As she lay in bed, the sounds of rain pattered on the rosebushes outside her window. Everything seemed to be thwarting her efforts, even nature. She would have to wait for this new storm to pass to go to Shrewsbury for it was several miles' walk and they had no conveyance.

Sleep proved elusive for her that night. Worries about Sir Evan and his reason for being there swirled about in her head. Was he as he appeared to be or was he a danger to her and the boys?

The offices of Mr. Albert Cornell were upstairs over a perfume shop just off Oxford Street near the heart of London. His skill and honesty in handling financial matters were excellent, and his clientele had grown over the years, affording him the means to move to better quarters. But he liked the cramped rooms, and the floral fragrance that often permeated the building.

On this morning, however, he wished he were anywhere but behind his desk, listening to the monstrous news that Lucinda, Dowager Lady Whitefield, had just imparted. How could this vain, silly creature have allowed that sweet child out during one of the worst storms of the spring? Sarah Whiting had been washed away from the Montford Bridge and lost downriver, or worse, drowned. Watching Lady Whitefield dab at her lovely eyes, he noted that not a tear had fallen on her lace handkerchief throughout her rather protracted saga. Was there more to this than appeared on the surface? After all, the girl was an heiress.

Cornell had kept tabs on little Sarah since her father died, per Phoebe Whiting's request. Lady Whitefield hadn't shown the least concern for the child, leaving her at school well past the normal time, never offering her a Season. But without a witness, other than her ladyship's oafish servant, he had little chance of proving foul play.

The widow interrupted his thoughts. "I am simply devastated, sir. Sarah and I had made such great plans for her to have a Season." The lady bent her head and her shoulders shook.

Little affected by what he deemed theatrics at best, the solicitor donned his glass, pulling a calendar toward him. "When did she disappear, my lady?"

"Tuesday, two weeks ago." Her tone held a very businesslike quality, as if they were getting to the part of the interview that most interested her.

Hand poised to write, he looked up, his brushy brows furrowing. "You waited a fortnight to inform me that I have a client missing? Madam, what can you have been thinking? I could have had men scouring the Severn's banks for her within twenty-four hours had I known."

The oaf beside her ladyship growled, "Her's dead. I seen her drown."

Cornell eyed the man with distaste, taking in the servant's frightful countenance and the badly cut clothes, which were new from the looks of them. "Then her body must be recovered. She needs a Christian burial. Besides, nothing can be done unless there is a body."

Lady Whitefield straightened. "What do you mean nothing can be done? I am the girl's only living relative. Barlow says she is dead." The lady fumbled in her reticule. She pulled out a folded document. "I insisted Sarah make out a will after you left. It states that I am her beneficiary, sir."

The solicitor sat back in his chair, not reaching for the will. It was all he could do not to laugh in the woman's face, but thoughts of Sarah in that cold river overpowered any satisfaction he had in knowing that this grasping female was not to have her way, for the present. "Lady Whitefield, by English law, unless there is a body to prove Miss Whiting is deceased, we must wait the standard seven years before any transfer of the estate."

"Seven years!" Her ladyship snapped. "Why that is ridiculous. We know she is dead."

"I know no such thing. In fact, I shall hire men to go and search for Sarah in case she's not—"

Lady Whitefield rose. "That won't be necessary. I shall set up a search at once. We shall find her body, sir. But don't think I shall employ you as my man of business, so disobliging as you have been." With that the lady swept from the room, the oaf in her wake slammed the door behind them.

Mr. Cornell waited a moment until the outer door banged with equal fury. He pondered the best action to take. He would set someone to look for Sarah and pray that they found something other than a body. But he wanted more. There was no question that something was havey-cavey about the dowager. He looked at the clock on the mantelpiece and decided that he would slip down to the Brown Duck for a bit of pigeon pie and a bumper of ale. It was likely he would have a late night. After coming to a decision, he rose and entered the outer office. "Frederic, is your cousin still living in Shrewsbury?"

The clerk peered over his half glasses. "Aye, sir.

Fiske works for the local vicar, keeping records and such."

"I should like to hire him for a week or so. We must find Miss Sarah Whiting, who disappeared off the bridge at Montford nearly two weeks ago during a storm. I want him to employ several men to look in every town between there and Bristol."

Frederic removed his glasses and began to clean them, not looking at his employer. "You know, sir, the likelihood is . . . well, she's not—"

"I know, but we must find something one way or the other." About to depart his office, he stopped. "And I would like to speak with a Runner as well."

Eyes wide, the clerk asked, "You think this is . . . foul play, sir?"

"That's what I want to know." Cornell took his hat from the rack. "I shall be back in thirty minutes. I shall take my supper and then return to do some work later." He exited his office, leaving Frederic agog at such shocking doings. Who would have thought that the Quality could be involved in murder?

It wasn't until the clerk heard the rain pattering on the street outside that he noted Mr. Cornell's umbrella still on the rack. Frederic grinned and shook his head that a gentleman that could be so good at remembering all the little details of his clients could be so careless about his own well-being.

The carriage bowled along in busy Oxford Street traffic as Lady Whitefield demanded, "Barlow, we drive straight back to Montford through the night. I insist that you scour every inch of that river, ask at every town and hamlet, every cottage."

The groom's brows drew together. "Ask what, my lady?"

The widow took her parasol and smacked her servant on the side of his grizzled gray head. "What have we been speaking of for the past two weeks? We must find Sarah. Ask if they have found a body. That solicitor won't give me the money without seeing her for himself."

A dawning lit the man's face and he nodded, then he pursed his lips. "Wouldn't things be easier if I dug up some young—"

Her ladyship shrieked, "Why must I be cursed with such a dolt to help me? Do *not* go anywhere near a cemetery, you fool, not unless you want to dance at the end of a rope."

Barlow shook his head. "Ain't never learn to dance."

Lady Whitefield covered her face with her hands and muttered, "God, grant me patience."

For two days after Sir Evan's meeting with Mrs. Ward and her sons, spring rains deluged Shropshire. Nature's onslaught kept most residents indoors except for those who had the most urgent business. On the second day the baronet, restless and full of uncertainty about his role in this charade, decided to tour one of the many churches for which Shrewsbury was famous. St. Alkman's, being next door to the Mellow Monk Inn, is where he started. Yet scarcely fifteen minutes inside the old Norman church, he realized he couldn't concentrate. His thoughts kept returning to Mrs. Ward and her secrets, despite the beauty of the stained-glass windows and the young curate who'd offered to be his guide.

The gentleman apologized to the clergyman, then stalked out of the building to stroll aimlessly through the streets of the town, ignoring the misting raindrops. With no destination in mind, he walked the narrow streets, coming upon the old Norman castle, which once had been the centerpiece of the town. Yet even that remarkable building did little to distract him from his worries and he continued to wander through the town. He found himself at the Quarry, which was something of a marketplace for Shrewsbury but there were few people braving the mud and rain. The town was situated on a hill overlooking a strange horseshoe bend in the river, and the citizens had taken full advantage of the unique terrain by creating a promenade along the Severn's edge. Drawn to the storm-tossed waters, he strolled along beside the river, debating the merits of what he'd set out to do for Titus.

Sir Evan halted near the bottom of the hill, watching the few brave fishermen who had taken their small boats onto the choppy waters. There seemed to be a great deal of activity on the boats, the steady rain seemingly not affecting their work. The baronet wished he could say the same about his mission. Titus was returning to Longdale with his wife in a scant two weeks and would expect to learn the truth, but Sir Evan had learned little during his one meeting with the lady. All he was certain of was that he detested the subterfuge. Yet he feared he, too, would be banned from the Wards' presence if he owned up to his relationship with the earl. He had little choice but to continue as he'd started, by trying to win their trust.

About to leave, Sir Evan started when a grizzled giant stepped into his path. The man's frightful countenance was unnerving, but it was his eyes that gave the gentleman a chill. They were like the cold unfeeling eyes of a fish.

"Beggin' yer pardon, sir. Have ye heard anythin' about a body washin' up on these here banks? Me daughter's gone missin' since that last frightful storm."

Sir Evan looked away from the man, ashamed of his revulsion. Even this unfortunate man had people who were important to him despite his appearance. "I'm sorry, but I haven't heard anything about a body being found. Perhaps you should ask those fishermen. I suspect they are here daily and would know of such."

With a bob of his head, the hideous giant moved farther down the banks to begin a shouted conversation with the men in the boats.

As the baronet watched the man lumber away, having no luck in his quest, he marveled at the giant's devotion. From the looks of him, the man could ill afford to be wandering about looking for his daughter, yet here he was searching when there would be little hope. Could the parent-child bond be that binding? His own father had been a cold, autocratic parent who had taught his son little about emotions. Then Sir Evans delved into the distant past and dredged up memories of his mother. She had been different, and he thought of her with great affection. Unfortunately, she'd died when he was but seven, and his father had gone a long way to dampen most of his son's tender feelings, considering them a weakness in a man. If his mother still lived would the ties of familial devotion cause him to want her close at hand as Lady Longmire wanted her mother?

The question released a flood of emotions for a gentle, caring woman. A woman he'd loved without reservation, and who'd loved him with equal devotion. For the first time in years, Sir Evan's throat tightened. He truly understood why the new countess might want her mother nearby. Surely Mrs. Ward would sympathize, being a mother herself.

Yet even as that thought came, the memory of the strange conduct of the boys at the cottage made him wonder if the Wards were hiding something. Did Cassandra Ward have a notorious reputation as a stage actress and had the boys been made aware what a shameful profession she'd practiced? Why else were they avoiding both Mr. Joiner and Titus? There was only one way to find out the family's secrets and that was to gain Mrs. Ward's trust. For that he must be closer to Wild Rose.

A sudden gust of wind brought a new torrent of rain wafting over the river. Sir Evan pulled up the collar on his tiered cape and hurried along the promenade toward town and the shelter of the Mellow Monk. As soon as the weather cleared he would go to Titus's steward and see about finding something at Longdale.

The following day dawned sunny and dry, albeit the roads still held muddy reminders of the previous day's storm. The baronet set out early for Longdale and found the steward already in his office. He quickly explained what he needed, knowing the man was in Titus's confidence about why Sir Evan was in Shropshire.

The man shook his head. "I've nothin' you'd be wantin' to live in, sir."

"I was a soldier, Joiner. I'm quite used to living rough. I'll take anything down near the river."

The steward turned to look at the estate map on the wall. "Well, I have a place but—"

"Take me there."

The expression on the old man's face clearly showed he didn't think the cottage would be fit for a gentleman, but he grabbed his hat, exited the estate office, and called for a horse. The steward led the way back toward Shrewsbury, Sir Evan following in his curricle. Just before Wild Rose came into view, the estate manager turned up a small lane that disappeared into the woods.

"There it is, sir." Joiner gestured at the cottage at the end of the overgrown path as Sir Evan drew his curricle to a halt beside the steward. "Like I said, it ain't ready for a tenant. His lordship had other matters to attend and more valuable properties, so we've only just begun the repairs. But if it's close to Wild Rose ye want to be, this is the best place on the estate."

Most young bucks of the *ton* would have turned tail and run at the sight of the dilapidated building, but Sir Evan merely quirked an auburn brow. Having spent many a cold night in Portuguese huts with dirt floors and no windows, this ancient cottage with cracked windows and a sagging roof nestled between two great oaks looked quite usable. The best part was that he was scarcely half a mile from the lady that was the object of his quest. "It will do, Joiner. Hawks and I shall move in this afternoon."

The earl's man nodded his head. "I shall have the housekeeper at Longdale send down the things you'll need to set up proper housekeepin'—pots, utensils, crockery, and linens."

"Why, thank you, Joiner. Oh, and feel free to continue the repairs while we are in residence. It won't bother us in the least."

He bid the steward good day. As he bowled back up the lane, he couldn't help wonder how Hawks would take such Spartan quarters. Well, after all, the man had offered to drive him to Hades—he just hadn't realized that they would have to stay awhile. With a laugh, Sir Evan guided his vehicle west toward town.

Sarah tied the blue ribbon of the chip-straw bonnet under her right ear. She gave a dissatisfied sigh at her appearance in the looking glass. Mrs. Ward's pale blue dress with tiny white dots of flock was a little too tight across the bodice, and the scalloped hem exposed a bit more of her ankle than she would have liked. But the garment fit the best of the dresses from which she had to choose. She certainly didn't want to draw attention to herself, yet she had little choice.

The trip to Shrewsbury was necessary. While milk and butter were delivered twice weekly from the Longdale home farm, the basics such as flour, sugar, spices and meat must be purchased from town and their larder was almost bare. They had been able to get by with a hare Jamie shot, and a hen from their henhouse, but the main portion of their diet had been eggs and the fish the boys caught from the Severn. Only the night before Ronald had sworn they would grow scales if they ate any more and Adam argued that they were all more likely to cluck than speak. Peter, with his ever-fertile imagination, had suggested they could be called Chicfins, which had brought peals of laughter from everyone.

Smiling at the memory, Sarah took a last glance at the dress and remembered the old saw "Beggars could not be choosers." The gown certainly was an improvement on her gray school dress, which hadn't faired well in her wet, muddy journey down the river. Gathering a tatted blue reticule, she went in search of Jamie, who was to accompany her to town.

She found him in the rear parlor, dressed in his Sunday best, giving Ronald instructions to keep the boys indoors and not to answer the door for any reason if someone came. While Ronald started the younger ones playing games on the parlor floor, Jamie went to the mantelpiece and took down an inlaid ivory box. He removed a leather pouch, which he handed to Sarah. "You'll need this for the expenses. Everything we order can be delivered."

Her brows rose at the weight of the purse. "Should I limit the spending?"

"Oh, don't worry about that." Jamie gave an airy wave of his hand. "We receive a quarterly income from my mother's solicitor, a Mr. Valentine from Portsmouth."

Sarah was pleased to know that the boys weren't destitute, but wondered if the solicitor knew of Mrs. Ward's demise. Would the income cease were that news imparted? If only her own inheritance weren't six years away, all this worry could be put to rest.

Jamie and Sarah bid the boys good-bye, while Ronald held a protesting Percy in check, the dog wanting to go for the walk. The pair exited the garden and set out at a brisk pace. The afternoon was pleasant, without a hint of rain, which was just as well, since they had over an hour's walk to town. The recent rains had spurred the foliage and the road was lined with blue speedwell, ox-eye daisies, and white mayweed. The boy dashed ahead and gathered small stones, skipping them across the glassy surface of the river, which paralleled the twin ruts leading to Shrewsbury. When he grew tired of the game, he fell into step with Sarah and began to speak of his worries about his brothers' future.

Sarah did her best to reassure him, hoping that the letter she was about to post to Mr. Cornell would solve not only her immediate problems but the boys' as well.

They had scarcely gone a mile when the sounds of horses and a carriage could be heard approaching them from behind. They moved to the side of the road to allow the vehicle to pass and continued their progress, but the curricle slowed and drew to a halt.

Sarah's heart raced as she looked up into the scarred, but handsome face of Sir Evan. There was a speculative gleam in his green eyes as if he might read her very soul by the expression on her face.

"Good day, Mrs. Ward. I am delighted to see you are feeling well enough for a walk."

There was no use pretending she was out of curl. Sarah had seen the roses in her cheeks in the looking glass. She gave a cool nod of her head. "I am well, sir. How is Mr. Hawks's ankle?"

"He declares himself fit and insists on returning to his duties, such as they are, ma'am. Might I inquire if this stroll is merely exercise or have you a destination?" The gentleman smiled, showing even white teeth.

Not immune to his charm, Sarah looked down the road toward town, hoping to put an end to the weak feeling in her knees. "Shopping, sir, one of the annoying tasks my father used to say men cannot abide." She looked back at him before she added, "Pray, don't let us keep you from your drive."

"As it happens, I am on my way to Shrewsbury to shop as well. I need to stock up my new cottage. Won't you allow me to give you and"—he eyed the boy carefully as if searching his memory, then finding what he wanted, continued—"Jamie a ride? You can do me a great favor by directing me to the best stores."

A sinking feeling settled into Sarah's stomach since she'd never been to Shrewsbury and hadn't the least notion where to shop. All her doubts about Sir Evan returned, and she was about to refuse when she saw the eager look on Jamie's face as he scanned the line of the curricle and team. There could be little doubt he wanted to ride and in all honestly so did she, for the distance was no small thing. Surely so short a trip could do no harm and Jamie would know where they must go. "Why, thank you, sir, if it won't be an imposition?"

Without further bidding, Jamie scrambled into the vehicle. "A bang-up set of goers you have, sir."

"Have you a fondness for horses?" Sir Evan leaned round the boy to assist Sarah into the vehicle. She settled into the curricle and the conversation moved to the finer points of blood lines and the breeding of prime cattle. Despite the baronet's injured hand, Sarah noted that he handled the ribbons with skill. They moved along the road at a steady speed, and Sarah began to relax and enjoy the ride, admiring the passing cottages and scenery. Then Sir Evan grabbed her complete attention with an unsettling statement.

"If you should like I can give you and your elder brothers driving lessons."

"Like!" Jamie crowed. "I should say so. Why that would be—"

"Sir Evan," Sarah interrupted the lad's raptures over such a treat, "that would be far too much trouble for you. After all you have your work here." She hated the crestfallen look on Jamie's face, but the one thing they didn't need was the gentleman spending time at Wild Rose and asking questions.

"Oh, 'twill be no trouble since I like to go out for a daily drive when I finish my research anyway. Besides I am your new neighbor at Twin Oaks Cottage, scarcely a half mile from Wild Rose. Shall we begin the first lesson at once?" He slowed the carriage to a halt and after some instructions handed the reins to Jamie.

But Sarah paid little attention to the lesson. Sir Evan was living in the cottage beside them. Could that just be a coincidence? Perhaps. Then she reminded herself of the conclusions she'd reached just before dawn. They had no proof against the gentleman and worry was useless. She would simply have to keep a close eye on him until Mr. Cornell came and she had other options. After all, both she and Jamie might be wrong about the baronet. He might be exactly what he claimed to be.

While Jamie drove, Sir Evan made occasional suggestions to his pupil. Just before they reached the bridge into Shrewsbury, Sir Evan took over the reins again, saying that town traffic and beginners were never a good combination.

"How did I do, sir?" Jamie asked.

"Excellent, my boy. I see a legend in the making," Sir Evan teased, then winked at Sarah over the lad's head.

The gesture gave her a warm feeling. She couldn't help but admire Sir Evan's patience with Jamie. How could such a man be anything but honorable? With that she pushed her doubts aside and determined to enjoy her outing. After all, he knew nothing other than that she was Mrs. Cassandra Ward, a respectable widow.

Shrewsbury was a bustling town that drew large crowds to market to purchase Welsh cottons, friezes, and flannels. Thankfully, this wasn't market day, so

Sir Evan guided the curricle easily through the streets, pointing out the churches he intended to study as they crossed the river into town—the towering spires of St. Mary's and St. Alkman's, the square Norman architecture of St. Julian's, the massive hulk of St. Chad, and the small quaint St. Giles. Following Jamie's directions, he drew to a halt in front of Harper's Emporium.

While the gentleman found a lad to hold his team, Sarah shoved the letter and a coin into Jamie's hand. "Go put this in the post while I do the shopping. Hurry back." Despite her growing confidence that the baronet was harmless, she wanted her affairs kept private.

The boy didn't question her; he merely slipped away while Sir Evan was distracted. When the gentleman joined her, glancing about for young Master Ward, she merely said, "Jamie had an errand to run. Shall we go in and do our shopping?" For a moment, she thought she saw a mixture of wariness and curiosity in his eyes, then he smiled and stepped forward, opening the door for her and to her relief, asking no prying questions.

The shop smelled of exotic spices. Sarah was able to fill her order with little difficulty, giving instructions for all to be delivered to the cottage. She even selected a variety of sweetmeats for the boys, as a treat. Sir Evan, quite unused to shopping, was wandering about picking up items and putting them down, unable to decide what he needed. With an exasperated grunt, he turned and asked for her assistance as he stood in front of barrels of spices. After several pertinent questions regarding Hawks's skill as a cook, she helped him select the basics needed to run a house. It took nearly thirty minutes

to finish and Jamie was waiting for them beside the
grays outside, chatting up the lad who held them.

When everyone was once again in the curricle,
Sir Evan asked, "Where to?"

Sarah announced she needed to visit the butcher,
the greengrocer, and finally the miller. The gentleman followed Jamie's directions and they soon had
placed orders at every shop, with each promising to
deliver their goods by the end of the day.

Standing in front of the miller's, Sir Evan pushed
his hat back slightly, making his auburn hair glint
with copper lights in the sunshine. "I had no idea
what a task shopping could be."

Sarah couldn't help but grin. "I told you that men
very often found it disagreeable."

"I would never call spending a day with a beautiful lady disagreeable, Mrs. Ward."

Sarah's cheeks warmed, and she turned to look
down the street, pleased at the compliment despite
everything. "Thank you, sir." But at that moment
her gaze caught a familiar face in the crowd and she
froze.

"Jamie, what say you to an ice, if you and your
mother have the time?" the gentleman asked the
lad, but his gaze was riveted on the mother's face.

Sarah, unaware she was being observed, couldn't
make her mind work properly as she watched the
hideous face of Barlow. His head and shoulders
were visible above the shoppers and he was coming
down the street toward her. He hadn't spotted her
as yet, but unless they left at once, he would pass
right beside her.

Seeing the horrified expression on the lady's face,
Sir Evan glanced in the direction she was staring.
One could scarcely miss the giant lumbering
through the crowded street. "Mrs. Ward, he is harm-

less I assure you. He is looking for his daughter who was lost during a storm."

Sarah's blue gaze flew to the baronet's concerned face. How did he know Barlow and what was this nonsense about a lost daughter? Lucinda's servant had never been married. Sarah lifted a trembling hand to her head. Barlow was looking for her and there was little doubt why.

Jamie stepped to her side. "Are you quite well . . . Mother?"

She gripped the boy's hand. "I have the headache. I must return home at once. Would you be so kind, Sir Evan?"

The baronet sprang into action, helping her into his curricle. Without a word, he urged his team forward, his face a picture of concern. Sarah couldn't resist taking one last glance over her shoulder. In that instant her gaze locked with the cold stare of her stepmother's groom and a chill raced down her spine. It was clear he'd seen her. As the curricle drew away from the curb, Barlow barreled down the street as fast as his hulking body and the milling shoppers would allow.

Bemoaning her discovery, Sarah turned her back to her pursuer and prayed that he wouldn't be able to find her since the cottage was so far out of town. Feeling a strange sense that she was being watched, she discovered Sir Evan's gaze on her and there was more than concern in his green eyes. There were questions as well. She lifted a hand to her face, to shield her from his prying gaze, and by the time they reached Wild Rose her head had begun to hurt for real.

Barlow halted in front of the miller's, gasping for breath. He wasn't as young as he used to be and that short run had left him winded. So that horrid child had survived the waters of the Severn. He could almost believe it was witchcraft. A shudder wracked him, sorcery being the only thing he truly feared. It stemmed from his mother having sworn a curse had been put upon her afore she delivered him, making him as he was.

Then his thoughts turned to his mistress. Her ladyship would not be well pleased with his news. Worse, he didn't know where the chit was staying. Envisioning the scene, he determined it might be best to stop at every house along the road to London, than to return home with no word of where the girl might be. That thought locked in his small mind, he set out in the direction the carriage had taken, a determined look on his freakish face making several people draw aside in alarm.

We'd Like to Invite You to Subscribe to Zebra's Regency Romance Book Club and Give You a Gift of 4 Free Books as Your Introduction! (Worth $19.96!)

If you're a Regency lover, imagine the joy of getting 4 FREE Zebra Regency Romances and then the chance to have these lovely stories delivered to your home each month at the lowest price available! Well, that's our offer to you and here's how you benefit by becoming a Regency Romance subscriber:

- **4 FREE** Introductory Regency Romances are delivered to your doorstep (you only pay for shipping and handling)

- 4 BRAND NEW Regencies are then delivered each month (usually before they're available in bookstores)

- Subscribers save almost $4.00 every month

- You also receive a **FREE** monthly newsletter, which features author profiles, discounts, subscriber benefits, book previews and more

- No risks or obligations...in other words, you can cancel whenever you wish with no questions asked

Join the thousands of readers who enjoy the savings and convenience offered to Regency Romance subscribers. After your initial introductory shipment, you receive 4 brand-new Zebra Regency Romances each month to examine for 10 days. Then, if you decide to keep the books, you'll pay the preferred subscriber's price, plus shipping and handling.

It's a no-lose proposition, so return the FREE BOOK CERTIFICATE today!

Say Yes to 4 Free Books!

Complete and return the order card to receive this $19.96 value, ABSOLUTELY FREE!

If the certificate is missing below, write to:
Regency Romance Book Club
P.O. Box 5214, Clifton, New Jersey 07015-5214
or call TOLL-FREE 1-800-770-1963
Visit our website at www.kensingtonbooks.com.

FREE BOOK CERTIFICATE

YES! Please rush me 4 Zebra Regency Romances (I only pay for shipping and handling). I understand that each month thereafter I will be able to preview 4 brand-new Regency Romances FREE for 10 days. Then, if I should decide to keep them, I will pay the money-saving preferred subscriber's price for all 4...that's a savings of 20% off the publisher's price. I may return any shipment within 10 days and owe nothing, and I may cancel this subscription at any time. My 4 FREE books will be mine to keep in any case.

Name _____

Address _____ Apt. _____

City _____ State _____ Zip _____

Telephone ( ) _____

Signature _____
(If under 18, parent or guardian must sign.)

RN082A

Five

Sir Evan stood inside Twin Oaks Cottage, surveying his new home with Hawks beside him. The valet's face held a resigned set. Having brought the ailing widow and her son home, the gentleman had returned to the Mellow Monk to retrieve his belongings and his servant to relocate all to the cottage in the woods. Unlike Wild Rose, which had been built for the long-ago earl's mistress, Twin Oaks Cottage was a tenant domicile and lacked the amenities of his nearest neighbor. There was a large front room with a newly installed flagstone floor that served as kitchen, parlor, and dining area. A loft with a straw mattress was over one end of the large room. A door on the back wall opened on a small chamber with a crude wooden bed. At the far end of the rear wall a smaller door opened to the woods that led to Wild Rose.

Hawks dropped the bags to the floor, causing eddies of dust to swirl up into the light. "I hope the lease was reasonable, sir."

Sir Evan laughed. "Most reasonable; in fact, the place is free." Noting several overturned chairs, he continued. "Shall I stay and help put things to rights?"

A wounded expression settled on the valet's face. "I ain't too old to do my duties yet, sir."

"Then I shall return in time for supper. I need to ask Mr. Joiner some questions about our mysterious Mrs. Ward."

The servant merely nodded, his thoughts already set on what needed to be done first. "If the things you ordered arrive today, I shall have your meal prepared by six." With that he picked up the gentleman's bags and moved toward the bedchamber.

Sir Evan returned to his curricle and set out for Longdale at a modest pace, his mind trying to puzzle out the day's events. The strange incident in Shrewsbury weighed heavily in his thoughts. What had frightened Cassandra Ward so mightily on the street in front of the miller's? At first he'd put the cause on the shocking appearance of that hideous man he encountered down by the river, but how could that be? What he'd seen in the lady's lovely face had been more than revulsion. There had been genuine fear. He knew that look well. He'd seen it enough in the men of his unit as they'd faced a French column marching over a hill.

Despite her claims of the headache, Sir Evan was convinced there had been something more. Something that hinged on her mysterious past, but what? It left him feeling frustrated at how little he knew of the lady, and so he'd made up his mind to question Joiner, the one man who might have some ideas.

Once again he found the burly steward ensconced in his office, working on the accounts. After a terse greeting, he put several questions to the man about the Wards.

Joiner put down his pen and shrugged. "Like I says to his lordship, there ain't much I can tell ye.

I was ordered to make Wild Rose ready for a new tenant last summer, and then his lordship drives away for nearly a month. The only reason I know the widow came from Portsmouth was from the Earl of Shrewsbury. I shared a tankard with his man at the Golden Hen Tavern, and he mentioned his master had seen Lord Longmire at a theater there while having his yacht refitted. Said he had a raven-haired beauty with him. Next thin' I know Longmire returns and announces her arrival the following day. Right sickly she was. Could scarcely descend from her carriage without her man's help. Been in bed ever since, as far as I know."

"It seems she's better. I discovered her and the eldest boy walking to town this morning."

Joiner frowned. "Strange."

The baronet smiled. "Do not people travel by foot in Shropshire?"

The steward leaned back in his chair, a thoughtful expression on his face. "Of course they do, sir. But my old mother spend two months in bed with an ailment once. The woman could scarce walk to the front door and back for weeks. Her limbs were weak as a kitten's. Our Mrs. Ward spends six months in bed, and then is able to walk several miles to town her first week up and about."

Sir Evan shrugged. "No doubt she has been improving steadily." Yet even as he defended her, he thought that an odd thing. His own recovery after his wounds had been slow, having lost a great deal of his strength from being bedridden. The mystery only seemed to be deepening.

"She was still abed when I saw her last week, sir. Her son said she was still too ill to see me." The man shook his head. "I had to insist. Truth be told, I would have sworn it wasn't the same lady I saw on that first day. Perhaps she was that much improved in her bearin', but I cannot say I got much of a look at her on her arrival."

The baronet rose, realizing that he would find no help here. "It seems no one but her boys and her servant know anything about the lady. Thank you, Mr. Joiner."

Sir Evan bid the man good day and set out for the cottage. As he came back parallel to the river, he drew his curricle to a halt and pondered the situation. He had to get closer to Mrs. Ward if he was to find anything out, but he wasn't sure even that would make her lift the veil of secrecy that shrouded her life. Perhaps he should request his own solicitor to find out what he could about the lady's affairs. He would write the man tonight. That decided upon, he set out for Twin Oaks Cottage.

He arrived back at the small structure and found his servant had done wonders with their new quarters. The main room was swept clean, the table and chairs strategically positioned in front of the fireplace. Hawks was in the process of making a lamb stew at a low-slung cupboard that could be used to as a worktable. Noting the pots, crockery, and utensils, Sir Evan was grateful to the Longdale housekeeper.

"Mr. Joiner sent the stuff, sir, along with fresh bedding and a few bits of furniture for your bedchamber. The footman said if there be anything else we need, to ask."

Hawks poured the gentleman an ale in a pewter mug, which he declared to be an excellent brew. The baronet sat in one of the crude chairs and sipped from the cup, trying to decide his next move after he'd written the solicitor. For a moment he watched his servant chop potatoes. Causally he confided the odd incident in town and his subsequent conversation with Joiner.

The old man kept busy, listening with interest. When the baronet finished, Hawks's brow puckered. "Afraid, was she? And you don't know about what?" The servant stopped what he was doing as he awaited an answer.

"All I could see out of the ordinary was this rather grotesque-looking giant of a man whom I met yesterday by the river searching for his missing child. Lost her in the river, he said. He was a coarse fellow with a face that could scare two years' growth from a child, but nothing to strike such fear into a grown woman. Especially one who has coped with as much as the widow has."

Hawks dumped all the cubed potatoes into the pot bubbling over the fire before he turned and looked at the baronet. " 'Tis all too mysterious for me. You'd need to ask my twin brother for a solution to this puzzle, him being the brains of the family. It's the only way anyone, save our ma, could ever tell us apart."

Sir Evan had briefly met his servant's brother and had remarked on their identical appearance. He'd seen nothing in Nick Hawks to make him think the man was extraordinary in any way, but he did own that not everyone could successfully manage a stable, which Nick appeared to do. "So, if my servant starts to suddenly know all the answers to my questions, I shall know you've pulled a switch on me so that you might run off for a holiday at the shore." Sir Evan grinned.

Hawks retrieved a spoon from the table, a twinkle in his brown eyes. "You needn't worry. I hate the seaside, makes me rheumatism ache. But for a lark me and Nick used to trade places all the time as youngsters. It's easy to fool people since they see what they expect to see."

The servant stepped back to the pot and began to stir as a thoughtful expression settled on Sir Evan's face. The baronet was suddenly reminded of something Joiner had said. The man claimed he couldn't even be sure the lady who'd arrived six months ago and the lady Sir Evan had met were the same woman. With so few people knowing Mrs. Ward, it would be easy to substitute another person and there was certainly motive. Wild Rose Cottage was a tenancy for life, according to Titus.

Then he laughed out loud, making the batman cum valet look at him in surprise. Even if Cassandra Ward had a twin sister, which was unlikely, she would never be willing to give up her own life to play nursemaid to seven children. The idea was ludicrous. He rose and picked up a bucket beside the table. "I shall bring some water to wash up for supper."

As the servant watched his master exit the cottage and head for the well, he couldn't help but be pleased. This little mystery Lord Longmire had dropped in the gentleman's lap had gone a long way to restoring Sir Evan's spirit for life. There was a part of Hawks that hoped a solution wouldn't be found too soon.

Sarah lay on the bed in Mrs. Ward's room, a sick feeling in her stomach. Barlow was close at hand. He knew she hadn't drowned in the river. She'd thought herself safe, but all that was past. Her first instinct was to flee to London, to find Mr. Cornell in person. There could be no doubt that Jamie would loan her the money from the household account. But she couldn't leave the boys here alone, and she couldn't risk taking them with her. What if Phillips or Joiner returned and found the place empty? Her one hope was that Barlow would never find the cottage, it being so far from Shrewsbury.

A scratching sounded on the door and Jamie's head appeared through the opening after she'd called for him to enter. "May I come in?"

She sat up and nodded. "Pray do, I need to speak with you."

The boy crossed the room and climbed up on the bed, where she patted for him to be seated. "Something happened today, Sarah. I can see it in your eyes."

She was constantly amazed at his innate acuity about his surroundings. "I have never told you about how I came to be in the Severn that horrible day."

"I always knew you would." He waited patiently for her reply, never probing for more than she was willing to offer.

The trust in his eyes overwhelmed her and reinforced her determination to stay and help. "My stepmother's servant threw me in the river." In a quiet voice she repeated the tale. She noted the flash of anger in the boy's dark eyes and she put a calming hand on him as she continued. "Today I saw that man in Shrewsbury. I am certain he saw me."

The lad slid off the bed, his arms akimbo, his body rigid with indignation. Yet one black curl dangling at his forehead ruined the effect, reminding her he was but twelve years old. "I have my father's pistol. He shan't hurt you again. I shall see to that."

"Jamie, there is no need to worry." She said the words, but knew that her own fears were far from over. "Barlow only saw me from afar. He doesn't know about this cottage. I feel certain I am safe.

Why, there are too many cottages and houses between us and where he spotted me for him to ask at them all. I am certain that he won't come here."

"But what if he does?"

Sarah bit at her lip a moment, then smiled. "You have done a wonderful job of keeping Lord Longmire and Mr. Joiner from seeing your mother. Can you not keep Barlow from seeing me?"

Jamie grinned. "He'll never know there's a lady in our house."

Morning came and with it Sir Evan rose even more determined to discover the truth about those living at Wild Rose. After breakfast he informed his servant that he intended to walk the distance to their neighbors. Hawks pointed out a path that led through the woods that would cut out nearly half the distance.

The gentleman put the letter he had penned to his solicitor the night before on the table. "I need you to go to Shrewsbury some time this morning to post this for me."

"Can it wait until I've finished doing a few errands here, sir?" Hawks lifted an ax and gestured toward the woods.

"There is no rush as long as it reaches the post office today." Sir Evan set out through the woods, wondering if Mrs. Ward had recovered from her episode in town. He suspected that his best chance of finding out anything of worth about the family would be to befriend the children. Soon the steady sounds of rhythmic chopping sounded from behind him as his servant replenished the wood for cooking. Moving closer to Wild Rose, the chopping echo in the woods was drowned by the melodic tone of a pianoforte. The song was familiar, but he couldn't place the name. Then he heard the lady's voice, strong and sweet, and marveled at her talent. Her skill only heightened his suspicions that, indeed, she'd trod the boards at some earlier time as actress or singer, but there was little difference in women of that ilk.

The thatched roof of the cottage became visible and the baronet slowed his steps as he neared the edge of the clearing. Stopping beside a tree, he could see into the rear parlor through the open double doors, where the lady sat playing. The children were seated about the room like an audience in front of her. As he listened to her he realized she was singing one of those nonsensical nursery songs that children love. It was clear by the faces of her own children that they were enjoying the performance greatly.

At the end of the song, Mrs. Ward rose and performed a curtsy with a great flourish. The children stood and clapped just as audiences often did at Haymarket. Sir Evan was shocked by the theatrical nature of the lady's gesture. How could he doubt Titus's speculation that she was an actress who'd seduced his father into giving her this house? He wondered if there had been a marriage to a Captain Ward, or was that merely a story she'd told the children? Yet there was a part of him that couldn't put the lady he'd met into that mold. She'd been genteel and reserved—but then an actress might well be able to play such a part. His mind warred with the possibilities.

From his position beyond the stone fence he could just barely make out her words as she shooed the boys outside to play while she baked cakes for afternoon tea. The boys came pouring out of the

open glass doors into the garden, causing Sir Evan
to step back behind the oak where he stood. It
wouldn't do to be caught spying.

The Ward children exited by the rear gate, and
began a game of tag, running into the woods. Percy
suddenly put his nose to the ground and began to
track some unsuspecting creature. The trail led him
through the open gate and in a flash a hare darted
from behind a bush and raced madly into the woods
just beyond where Sir Evan stood. He held his
breath for a moment, fearing the dog might catch
his scent and set up to barking as he had before,
but the canine was too intent on the hare. He raced
past the gentleman's hidden position, bounding
into the woods in full flight.

Realizing that the time for revealing himself was
past and would now be awkward, Sir Evan turned
and slipped back toward the path that had brought
him to Wild Rose. Perhaps he would come later in
the day via the front door. He moved stealthily
through the woods until the sounds of the children's voices and laughter could scarcely be heard
through the dense trees.

Almost halfway back to Twin Oaks Cottage a
sound penetrated the woods that sent a chill down
Sir Evan's spine. He froze and looked about, but
could see nothing but trees, ferns, and low bushes.
Then his gaze lit on tracks in the damp earth.

A wild boar lived in these woods!

In an instant he knew he must get the children
out of the woods. He whirled and dashed back down
the path. Once again he could clearly hear the children's voices and followed the chatter.

Fear drove him and even before he caught sight
of them he shouted, "Jamie, take the children inside. There is a boar nearby." He broke through

the underbrush into a small clearing and discovered the children frozen, not seeming to understand the seriousness of what he'd called to them. His startling arrival appeared to be what had frightened them. He repeated, "There is a wild boar in the woods, you must all go back inside."

With shrieking that would have frightened even a banshee, the boys ran in the direction of the cottage. The last one hadn't left the clearing when a great tusked boar broke through the trees at the far end of the clearing, seemingly in hot pursuit. About to run to safety, Sir Evan realized that one small boy stood like a statue at the edge of the trees on the opposite side of the meadow, staring at the charging animal in terror.

Sir Evan bolted toward the boy as if he had wings on his feet, but even as he closed the gap, he could hear the animal bearing down on him. He scooped up the child and shoved him onto a nearby tree limb. But before he could save himself, he was knocked from his feet by the charging beast. Pain seared through him where the animal's ugly tusks gored him.

Still his thoughts were for the child. "Stay up there, boy." Sir Evan struggled to his feet, then staggered into the meadow to draw the beast away from the child. Turning to face the woods where the boar had disappeared, his injured leg gave way and he again collapsed. The sound of the hooves of the beast could be heard thundering back toward him. He managed to stand once again on his one good leg, but blood loss made him light-headed. As the animal broke from the underbrush, Sir Evan stood resolute, knowing he couldn't escape.

The report of a pistol on the opposite side of the clearing startled him. Only feet from where he stood, the boar went down hard in the meadow and grew still. A red rivulet streamed from his dark fur just behind his front leg. The baronet, growing weak, could see nothing but the cloud of black powder smoke, then Hawks stepped into the clearing. The servant ran to his master, who once again collapsed into the grass.

Sir Evan gasped out, "Go to the boy. Make certain he's unhurt."

"After I staunch this blood, sir." The valet pulled out the tail of his shirt, tearing a strip from the bottom, then knelt to make a tourniquet. The last thing Sir Evan saw before he was consumed by darkness was his man's face intent on his task.

In the kitchen at Wild Rose, Sarah was putting the apple tarts in to bake as the pistol shot jarred her from her task. The boys were in the woods! She slammed the iron door with a loud bang and raced out of the cottage. She'd barely taken two steps out the rear door when the boys came pouring out of the forest, terror etched on their faces, screaming in fear. They ran through the open gate into the rear garden straight into her arms. Relief flooded her to see them unharmed, but it took her several moments to discern what they were shouting. At last she realized that a boar had chased them from the woods.

Jamie, gasping for breath, said, "Sir Evan came to warn us and"—He froze as his gaze scanned the dark-haired lads crowded round Sarah. Horror hewed his young face. "Dear Lord, Luther is not with us." Without thoughts for his own safety, the boy dashed back toward danger.

"Stay here," Sarah barked to the others. With that

she picked up her skirts and followed after Jamie, praying that little Luther was unharmed. Jamie was so fast she lost sight of him in the thick undergrowth, but she could hear the pounding of his footsteps ahead. Fear and exertion made the blood pound in her ears as she ran. When she broke into a clearing she halted at the sight before her, even as she struggled to catch her breath. Sir Evan Beaumont lay on the ground, Hawks kneeling beside the man. Jamie was on the far side of the meadow, his arms extended to Luther, who was perched on a tree limb.

Realizing that the child was unharmed, she hurried to where the gentleman lay. His face was deadly pale and blood trickled from the makeshift bandage Hawks had wrapped round the leg wound. The servant rose, all his worries written on his weathered face. "It's awful bad, ma'am."

"Bring him inside Wild Rose."

Jamie came to her side, leading a sniffling Luther. He passed the boy's hand to Sarah. "If you will take Luther, I'll help Mr. Hawks move the gentleman to the cottage."

Sarah nodded, still watching the gentleman's pale face, hoping for him to awaken. "We must send for the doctor at once." Her gaze flew to Jamie, whose eyes widened at her announcement. He looked to the wounded man, taking in the bleeding leg. Resignation molded his young features into an adult mask. Sir Evan might die. They had no choice in the matter. The lad gave a terse nod of agreement.

The valet, unaware of the interplay between the woman and child, gave the lad instructions on how to lift Sir Evan. It took some ten minutes, but they finally had the baronet safely stretched out upon a worn daybed in the rear parlor. Sarah had hurried ahead and covered the blue damask daybed with a blanket. The younger boys crowded inside the doorway to the hall, whispering amongst themselves.

Jamie gave Hawks exact instructions on how to find the doctor in Shrewsbury. The old servant, about to depart, stopped and looked at the woman and boy. "Take care of him. He's had too much trouble for one lifetime."

Sarah, putting her arm about Jamie, said, "We will, Mr. Hawks." She could only wonder at such a statement of woe, but then she knew as little of Sir Evan as he did of her.

With a nod of his head, the servant departed for Twin Oaks Cottage to retrieve a horse to make the journey go faster. As the door closed, Ronald stepped from the group of brothers that surrounded him. "What shall we do about Dr. Bergen? He will know at once that you are not Mama."

Jamie looked at Sarah, then back at his brothers. "We have no choice. Sir Evan needs a physician. It would seem the truth is about to be revealed."

Seeing all the glum faces staring at her, Sarah put her arms around Peter and Alan, who had moved to stand beside her. "Don't lose faith, boys. I would never allow you to be sent to the workhouse, come what may." She could only hope that Mr. Cornell would be able to help her keep such a bold promise.

Good luck arrived at Wild Rose Cottage some forty minutes later that morning in the form of one Ian MacGregor, former surgeon in His Majesty's Army. Having sold out after Toulouse, he and his bride had returned to Shropshire to join his father-in-law, Dr. Bergen, and offer his services to the local citizens. While Bergen handled much of the illness,

MacGregor's specialty was dealing with wounds, and they found their joint practice mutually beneficial. Mrs. MacGregor was happy to be back with her widowed father in the town of her youth.

In his early thirties, with a lean freckled face, the Scotsman was as tight with his words as his money. With little more than a curt nod of his bushy red head, the doctor went straight to the patient, Hawks fast on the man's heels. MacGregor barked several orders at Sarah, then took off his coat and opened his black leather bag. Pulling up a chair, he began to unwrap the wound.

Sarah hurried to the kitchen and brought him water and clean linens. He absently thanked her, saying that would be all, as he inspected the wound.

"Perhaps you will be kind enough to leave Sir Evan's servant to help me, Mrs. Ward, since I must remove the gentleman's breeches," MacGregor announced as he began to unlace the gentleman's brown buckskins without so much as a glance at her.

Sarah's cheeks warmed and without a word she slipped from the room. She joined the boys in the front parlor, where she had sent them on the doctor's arrival.

Jamie rose and came to her as she entered the room. "How is Sir Evan?"

"He is still unconscious but the doctor is working on him." She paused and looked at her hands for a moment and was surprised to see how they trembled. Closing them into fist, she said, "I suppose the doctor was so distracted he didn't realize that I'm not your mother, for he addressed me as such."

A half smile tipped the boy's mouth. "*He* has never met Mama. Only Dr. Bergen ever visited, so we are safe for the present." He grew solemn again.

"If only Sir Evan were well, I should be quite happy."

Sarah agreed with him fully. There could be no explaining it, but she had grown quite fond of the gentleman in the short time they'd known one another. He'd done a wonderful thing in saving young Luther's life. She prayed he would return to good health soon.

In the rear parlor some thirty minutes later, Dr. MacGregor sat back and looked at the tight bandage he'd made over the jagged flesh. "That should do it, laddie." He spoke as if his patient might hear him.

Hawks, watching over the man's shoulder, gave a grunt of approval. He'd seen many a battlefield surgeon work and this one seemed to know his profession well. The wound appeared to have stopped bleeding. "Do you think he'll be all right, sir?"

The doctor seemed to come out of some deep trance at the question. His red brows flattened into a straight line as he plunged his hands into the bowl of water to wash them. "If infection doesn't set in and you can keep the laddie still for the next week or so, I think all will be well." His brows relaxed. "But truth be told it's in God's hands, like much of my work."

Hawks was a soldier. He'd seen many a man succumb to the aftereffects of a wound, and he was determined that wouldn't happen. In his mind cleanliness was the key. If he had to use every strip of linen in Shropshire he would change the dressing every day.

The doctor interrupted the valet's thoughts. "I must speak with the lady of the house. She will need to have instructions on what to do for her guest."

A moan rose from the patient, grabbing both

men's attention. Sir Evan's eyes slowly opened and there was a moment of dazed disorientation before he focused on a face he recognized. "I . . . don't seem . . ." His green eyes widened even further as his memory seemed to return. "I—is the boy unharmed?"

"Aye, sir, he's with his brothers all in one piece, which is more than I can say for you."

The gentleman attempted a smile, but his face evolved into a grimace of pain, and he again closed his eyes as if all his strength had been sapped by the question. The doctor silently signaled Hawks to go and find Mrs. Ward, before sitting back in the chair beside his patient.

"Name's MacGregor, Sir Evan. Your wound is serious and you must follow my instructions exactly. Any further bleeding and I cannot make any promises about how all will turn out." He paused a moment, studying the baronet's scarred face. "But then I see you must be familiar with gentlemen of my profession."

Sir Evan's eyes opened after several minutes and he gave a nod of his head. "Too familiar as you can see."

Before the doctor could respond, Hawks opened the door and ushered the mistress of Wild Rose into the parlor.

Sarah stepped into the room and relief rushed through her to see Sir Evan looking, if not healthier, at least aware of his surroundings. The doctor rose and came to her, distracting her from his patient.

"Ah, Mrs. Ward, 'tis a pleasure to meet you, I believe it was my father-in-law who had the honor of treating you upon your arrival." As he spoke, his brows seemed to flatten as if there were something about that which puzzled him.

Frightened at the subject of Cassandra Ward's health, Sarah said, "But as you can see, sir, I am much recovered."

"Fully, it would seem." A speculative gleam came into the doctor's eyes for a moment.

Hoping to turn his thoughts in another direction, Sarah asked, "How is Sir Evan?"

Dr. MacGregor turned to his patient, who was looking at his hostess. "For the present he is well. I fear that you shall have a guest for some time. I don't want to risk his leg bleeding again by moving him, not even from this parlor for the moment."

"I understand." Sarah's heart seemed to skip a beat at the prospect of being in such close quarters with the gentleman.

Their gazes locked and she was startled to see that he seemed as pleased as she by the turn of events.

"I apologize for the inconvenience to your household, Mrs. Ward." The gentleman's voice appeared frighteningly weak to Sarah. It reminded her that they were far from out of the woods on his recovery.

"It is a small thing, sir, compared to what you did for Luther and the other boys. We could never do enough to repay you."

Dr. MacGregor picked up his bag. "Excellent. I am leaving a bottle of laudanum for you to use for the pain and to help you sleep. I shall come again tomorrow, sir. You must get as much rest as possible." He waited until Sir Evan closed his eyes, then turned to Hawks and Sarah and began to give them detailed instructions about the care of his patient. About to depart, the doctor eyed the loyal servant thoughtfully. "Do not try to do all the work yourself, or I shall be here treating you, my good man. Mrs. Ward and her elder boys can do much to help with Sir Evan's care. No sitting up all night for either of you. You can do part and the lady can do part. Understand?"

The old servant nodded as he exchanged a glance with Sarah. She knew that while he said he agreed, she would have to push him to rest. There was a great deal of affection for his master evident in the worry on his worn face.

About to depart, the doctor halted and directed his question to the servant. "Did you kill the boar?"

"Aye, sir." Hawks sounded well pleased with himself.

MacGregor arched one red brow. "Then you might want to inform Lord Longmire's steward. I shouldn't want to learn you'd been thrown in the gaol for poaching, and you shouldn't allow the meat to go bad. If Joiner don't want it, the local orphanage could put it to good use."

"No worry about that, sir," the valet said gruffly as he looked to where his master lay, seemingly asleep on the daybed.

The doctor grinned. "Then I suppose it shall be roast boar for supper, Mrs. Ward."

Placing his black beaver hat on his bright red hair, he bid them all good day, but Sarah scarcely paid much heed. Her thoughts were riveted on Hawks's final statement. Why was there no such worry? She knew the laws about killing animals on private lands were very stringent. One needed permission to hunt and kill on another man's estate. Was Hawks merely confident that Lord Longmire would understand the circumstances or was there something more?

"Mrs. Ward?" Hawks interrupted her musing. "If you will sit with Sir Evan, I shall go and bring some of the gentleman's things over from Twin Oaks."

"Yes, oh yes, I shall stay beside him until you return."

After one final glance at the sleeping man, Hawks quietly exited the room. Sarah moved to the chair beside the daybed, taking in every feature of the baronet's face. An urge to stroke away the lines of pain that surrounded his mouth welled up in her and she entwined her fingers to keep herself from such a liberty. What was this strange fascination she had for the gentleman? She turned her gaze out the window, trying to regain her sense of propriety.

When at last she looked back, Sir Evan had fallen asleep. His chest rose and fell in a deep rhythm, which was a comforting sight. The doctor had said sleep was important. She leaned over and tugged the blanket up to his shoulders. Sitting back, she was torn about having him in the household. On the one hand she knew it was their duty to take care of him and she gladly would. In the depths of her heart she knew she would even enjoy his company. Still his presence increased the risk that her masquerade would be exposed and thereby endangering the boys' future. It was going to be a long and arduous week ahead.

Six

Sarah tugged the Norwich shawl tighter about her shoulders but it had little to do with holding off the night chill. Fear had taken hold of her. Nearly twelve hours had passed since the accident and Sir Evan lay on the daybed shivering with chills and fever, which, as Hawks had told her only moments before he departed on an errand, did not bode well. It was likely a sign that infection had set into the wound. The laudanum Dr. MacGregor had given the baronet earlier made him sleep much of the afternoon, but he'd awakened near seven o'clock, his cheeks flushed and his eyes bright. They'd scarcely been able to make him take a little broth and some wine, then he'd again fallen asleep.

Busy with getting the boys ready for bed, Sarah had left the gentleman under the watchful care of Hawks for much of the evening. She even went to bed for a while, but worry had kept her awake. With little hope of sleeping, she rose and dressed. Going to the parlor, she'd offered to relieve the gentleman's servant for several hours. Surprisingly, the man agreed without protest, saying he had an errand to run. As she sat beside the patient, Sarah wondered what errand Hawks must do this late at night.

Restless, Sir Evan mumbled in his sleep. She could make out bits of what he was saying. Such words as "advance," "hold fast," and "flank the enemy," told her he was reliving his war experiences. As the hands of the clock moved closer to midnight he grew more agitated, trying to push off his blanket.

Deciding to bathe his face with lavender water to cool him so he would fidget less, she sat on the edge of the daybed. She used the compress that was soaking in a bowl on the nearby table. As she touched his forehead with the damp cloth, his eyes flew open but there was a dazed look in their emerald depths. He stared at Sarah, uttering a hoarse whispered, "Violet?"

"No, Sir Evan, it is . . ." Sarah hesitated to give the false name to the sick man.

In the silence of the delay, he moaned, "Oh, Violet, why?" Before Sarah could utter another word, the gentleman grasped her arms and drew her down, pressing his fevered lips to hers. Her first instinct was to draw back, but despite the baronet's condition, his strength had not totally failed him. The kiss was heated and angry, but soon gentled to one of pure passion.

To her utter amazement, Sarah found her first kiss not an unpleasant experience. A strange tingling sensation seemed to race to every part of her, and she found herself relaxing into his embrace. Released at last as the gentleman's strength was spent, she drew back to gaze at him but he had once again fallen into a fevered stupor.

Her cheeks warmed with a guilty flush. She had no right to be enjoying a kiss that was meant for another. Leaving the damp compress on the gentleman's forehead, she moved back to her seat near the window. But she was full of questions. Who was

Violet and why did Sir Evan sound so hurt when he spoke her name? Had she betrayed him in some way? Did he love her so much?

Before she could ponder the questions for long, a knock sounded at the door. Ronald put his head through the opening and gestured for Sarah to come. She slipped outside the makeshift sickroom into the unlit hall, where the boy stood holding a flickering candle. "Is something wrong?"

"I heard you and Mr. Hawks talking early this evening about Sir Evan. He's feverish?"

She nodded. "He is getting worse."

"Here." He handed her a box. "I brought you this willow bark. Make it into tea and that will help bring down his fever. It always works."

Sarah took the box, then kissed the boy on his cheek. "Thank you, Ronald. I shall do so at once. Go back to bed and I shall see you in the morning."

She borrowed his candle to light one in the hall, then watched the lad climb the stairs back to his room. There was little doubt he would eventually make an excellent doctor. For him it wasn't just about the science, he truly cared about people. On that thought she hurried to the kitchen and used the water she'd left heating over a low banked fire. Returning to the parlor with the brewed remedy to which she'd added a bit of cool water to make it drinkable, she began the task of waking the gentleman enough to get the liquid in him.

Again he mumbled, but it seemed his thoughts were again on the woman. "Beautiful creature." Then he moaned, "An actress for certain."

This Violet seemed to have enchanted him. Feeling low at such a thought, Sarah lifted his head. "Sir Evan, you must drink this."

The man's eyes opened. "You are here?' There
was excitement in the tone of the announcement.

But she suspected that in the midst of his delirium
he was again seeing Violet. "Drink this, sir. It will
help."

He took several thirsty gulps of the tepid liquid,
then collapsed back onto the daybed, his eyes closing. "So weak. I cannot . . ."

Thinking he'd drifted off again as he failed to say
what he meant, Sarah put the cup on the nearby
table. His hand grasped her wrist and she looked
back to see him staring at her. "So beautiful." Then
his eyes closed and his fingers relaxed from her arm.

There was a part of her that very much wished
he were speaking of her. But she knew he was ill
and seeing things that weren't there. All his
thoughts were of Violet. Sarah again wet the compress and replaced it on his brow, then moved back
to the chair to wait and see if the willow bark tea
would help.

Some thirty minutes later the door to the parlor
opened and Hawks returned, carrying a small bundle. "How is he?"

"Decidedly feverish, but I managed to get him to
drink some medicinal tea."

"That should help." He went to the table and
unwrapped the bundle. "I'm going to put a salve
on the wound which my mother always used."

As the servant came near, Sarah detected a strong
odor and wrinkled her nose with distaste. "Are you
certain that is safe? It smells quite horrid."

Hawks grinned. "Always worked for us as boys.
It's the sulfur what makes it stink, but Ma always
swore that was what did the best." He handed her
the small pot, then lifted the blanket off the gentleman's injured leg.

Sarah, on seeing the long muscular limb, averted her eyes even as her heart seemed to race at the sight. To cover her nervousness she asked, "What else is in this mixture? I might want to use it with the boys."

"Equal parts sulfur and honey. 'Twas the honey that I had to go to Longdale to find." The man was unwrapping the wound and he didn't see the startled reaction to the name.

"L—Longdale! You went to the earl's house?" Sarah's heart began to race in earnest. A jumble of thoughts all seemed to be warring with one another about why he'd gone to the earl.

"Aye, ma'am. 'Twas the closest place I could think of at the moment. Didn't think his lordship would be wantin' one of his tenants to die of a wound inflicted by one of his own boars." He took the pot from Sarah and began to smear the potion on the angry-looking wound.

A sigh of relief escaped Sarah. That made sense. Her nerves seemed to be getting the best of her.

Hearing the lady sigh, Hawks looked up. "You must be tired, ma'am, what with all the work you must have takin' care of so many boys. Go to bed. I shall stay by Sir Evan."

"But you need your rest as well," she protested but she knew the boys would be up early expecting breakfast.

"Don't worry. I'll catch a few winks here in this chair. There's naught either of us can do until he improves." The servant began to rewrap the wound from the pile of fresh linen strips that Sarah had put on the table.

"Very well, but call me if you have need of me." With that she retired to her room. As she lay down for the night, her thoughts returned to Sir Evan's muttered words. Sarah didn't know who Violet was, but she couldn't deny that she owned a bit of envy for the unknown lady.

Near dusk the following day, the patient's fever broke. Sir Evan awoke with no memory of where he was in the dimly lit room. His thoughts were all a jumble, full of sights and sounds of the war, and he realized he'd been reliving his experiences in his nightmares. But Violet had been in his torment as well, and he'd kissed her, or had he? It had seemed like Violet, but the sweet scent of roses had made him wonder. His memory flashed on the beautiful widow there in the flesh. But his thoughts were still so muddled, he wasn't certain if he'd dreamed her by his side. He turned his head toward the window and spied Hawks dozing in a chair. The baronet didn't doubt his valet had been there for however long he'd been ill. The man was a good and loyal servant.

The sounds of children's chatter coming from the room across the hall brought the memories rushing back. The meadow in the woods. The boar. The children. Everyone save himself had escaped uninjured. He wondered how long he'd been on the daybed in Mrs. Ward's parlor. Had the accident happened only that morning?

He shifted his weight to rise to a sitting position, causing a sharp pain to race up his leg. The creaking of the old daybed awoke Hawks. In an instant he was out of his chair beside his master.

"Here, sir, let me put another pillow behind you." The servant's face owned a day's growth of gray stubble that looked like snow on his tanned skin.

Clearly it had been much longer than a mere day since the attack.

"H—how long have I been asleep?" Sir Evan croaked, his voice hoarse from lack of use.

The valet poured out a glass of water, which he handed to the gentleman. "The better part of thirty-six hours, sir. Feverish, too, but between me and Mrs. Ward, we brought you through it fine." Hawks then set about lighting more candles in the growing dusk, telling the gentleman that everything had been handled with the boar.

Sir Evan sipped the water despite his great thirst. He knew from his last convalescence that too much in the beginning would make him sick. So the young widow hadn't been a dream. A soft scratching sounded at the door and Hawks called for the visitor to enter.

As if his thoughts had conjured her, Cassandra Ward, looking beautiful in a blue sprigged muslin gown trimmed with white lace, stepped into the room. Her black hair was neatly bound into a chignon at the nape of her neck. The sedate style gave her a more mature look, but still she seemed far too young to be the mother of seven boys. A smile lit her face as she noted that Sir Evan was awake.

"I thought I heard voices as I passed by the door. How are your feeling, sir?"

"A bit shaky but I think on the mend. May I offer my thanks to you for all that Hawks tells me you have done?" Sir Evan wondered about another image that flashed in his thoughts. Had he kissed those lovely lips? Or had that too been part of his dreams, too?

"There is no need for such thanks, sir. Without you, Luther might have been killed. Are you hungry?"

About to say no, he knew that if he did, he was not likely to see Mrs. Ward again for a while. "I could use a little something to eat, but don't go to any great trouble."

"I made leek soup and fresh bread, if you should like a bit of that. Dr. MacGregor said once your fever broke you may have what you like." The lady smiled.

"That sounds excellent." Beside him he heard Hawks make a soft grunt, but Sir Evan never so much as flinched, only returned the smiled of the lady, whose own seemed to make something happen inside his chest.

"I shall only be a moment." The lady departed.

The door scarcely closed before the valet said, "Leek soup, is it? You've always detested such."

Sir Evan closed his eyes. "I couldn't be rude, Hawks. Besides, I can eat plenty of bread if I find it unpalatable."

Fussing with the strips of fresh linen, Hawks stopped and quirked a bushy brow. "Actually you may find the meal a surprise. Mrs. Ward is quite the cook. Her soup is done in the French style, lots of herbs and very tasty, if I may say so, sir."

"Has the lady made another conquest?" The gentleman's eyes opened and he smiled at his servant.

"Nothin' like that, sir. But she's been a proper hostess." The older man looked about to see that everything was neat and tidy, then he said, "If you don't mind, sir, now that you're awake, I'll just make a run to the necessary."

"I shall be fine. Take your time."

After his man left, Sir Evan lay quietly awaiting his meal. His thoughts drifted to the puzzle of Mrs. Ward. Everything about her screamed that she was a lady of breeding, yet Titus was convinced otherwise. But was his friend being fair? Or had his motives for getting the lady from the cottage blinded him to the true nature of his tenant? Still there was the mystery of why the old earl had given her the house. It was certainly a puzzle.

Some five minutes later, the lady, who seemed to dominate his thoughts, returned with a tray, Hawks at her heels. She'd added a pot of tea and fresh strawberry preserves to the meal. Hawks drew a small table near and she sat in a nearby chair and poured out his tea, offering him a napkin.

"When you are rested, Sir Evan—"

A knock sounded at the front door, interrupting whatever the lady had been about to say. Sir Evan was certain that he saw a flash of terror race across the woman's face before her gaze dropped to her hands, which she now held clutched in her lap. "Jamie will get that."

Listening to the boy in the hall, the baronet wondered what they feared so much at the cottage. While he was more and more convinced that Titus was wrong about the lady, there certainly was some mystery afoot. For the first time he realized that his wound might be fortuitous since he would have to stay for some time.

Moments later Dr. MacGregor entered the room. "Well, I see my patient is on the road to recovery at last." He then took Mrs. Ward's hand, bowing low and kissing it, which sent a strange surge of jealousy through Sir Evan. "My dear lady, I do apologize for calling so late, but there was an overturned cart in town this afternoon and I have just finished bandaging four local lads who fancied themselves whips. Thankfully it was just cuts and bruises."

After greeting the doctor, the lady of the house excused herself. "I shall be next door with the boys should you need anything."

The door closed behind her, and when the doctor turned to face his patient a slight frown puckered his brow.

"Is there some problem, Doctor?" Sir Evan asked.

" 'Tis only that I was speaking to my father-in-law this morning about our bonny Mrs. Ward. He treated her upon her arrival in Shrewsbury about six months ago. He was greatly surprised to hear of her complete recovery. It was his opinion that she'd stick her spoon in the wall within months, so ill did she seem." The man shrugged. "But then a great deal of what we do is educated guessing. Medicine is not an exact science, I fear." With a philosophical sigh he advanced to the daybed. "Ah, laddie, best let me take a look at that wound."

The doctor stayed only long enough to unwrap the wound, debate the value of Hawks's salve, and rebind the leg in clean linen. He determined that his patient was on the mend, but ordered him to stay quiet and not to set foot out of the cottage for at least several days. Urging him to eat his supper, MacGregor departed, promising to call at the end of the week to make certain his patient continued to improve.

Sir Evan eyed the soup hesitantly, then gave it a try. Hawks was right, it was perhaps the best the gentleman had ever tasted. Within minutes, he emptied the bowl and began putting inroads into the thick slices of bread. All the while, his mind kept returning to that look of fear that had flashed on the lady's face at the sound of the front knocker. What did Cassandra Ward fear? Or perhaps he should say whom?

The doctor's strange tale of a dying woman who seemed to be anything but only added to the deepening mystery at Wild Rose. But Sir Evan was more determined than ever to solve it. Only now he was at last in a position to find some answers. Yet instead of revealing what he would learn to Titus, he only wanted to help protect her and her boys.

With a shake of his head he reminded himself that he owed his life to Titus. His loyalties should remain with his friend. If only he could determine a way to do what was best for both of them. At the moment that solution seemed unattainable.

After he finished his meal, Sir Evan urged his servant to return to Twin Oaks and get a good night's sleep. "I shan't need anything further this evening."

Despite some protest, Hawks agreed to do as his master wished, since he needed to tend the horses. "But if you have need of anything, don't hesitate to call on Mrs. Ward." With that the servant departed taking the tray with him. Sir Evan lay on the daybed, more questions than answers filling his head until at last his body's demand for healing rest drew him into sleep.

Barlow slipped along the fence toward the large stone cottage. He was tired and the sun hovered behind the nearby trees but he had a mission to fulfill. He must find Sarah Whiting for Lady Whitefield. Through the open windows, the smell of baked ham and apple tarts wafted on the breeze, making his stomach grumble. It had been hours since his last meal, but he was determined to discover if the chit was hiding here. The neat cottage was the fourth place he'd stopped since leaving Shrewsbury. He'd gone in the direction he'd last seen the curricle that held Sarah, but so far all he'd gotten for his trouble was a dressing down by some old butler, the door slammed in his face by a shrieking maid, and the dogs set upon him by the master at the last house.

Well, he wouldn't be such a fool as to go to the front door this time. He'd take a peek in the window and see just who resided here. On reaching the north side of the building, he discovered the open window nearly two feet above his head. Inside he could hear the clatter of cutlery and conversation. Thinking everyone would be at table, he grabbed a hold of the thick ivy that clung to the walls and climbed slowly to the opening.

At the exact moment he popped his head above the jamb, a little maid carrying a large tureen came to the sideboard beside the window. On seeing what she would later describe as a monster at the window, she hurled the heavy crockery at his head.

The great dish seemed to hover in the air a moment before its hot contents washed down over Barlow's head, covering him with thick potato soup. A cacophony of screams sounded in the dining room, leaving the giant on the ivy with no other choice but to jump down and run blindly toward the woods. First he tripped over the tureen on the ground and then a rosebush, which inflicted its fury.

A voice shouted, "Bring me my gun, Albert."

Scraping the remains of the soup from his eyes, Barlow raced as fast as he could into the nearby trees. Despite his age and size he managed to go almost two miles before he had to stop from fatigue. Well away from the cottage, he gasped for breath and slowed to a meandering gait. He was too tired to walk back to Shrewsbury and would hardly be welcome at any inn in his condition. At last he found a small thicket where he could spend the night. He lay down on a bed of leaves beneath the trees, and gathered his thoughts.

Of one thing he was certain, Sarah had not been in that dining room. In the moments before he'd been souped, he'd seen several blond-haired young ladies, a mother whose red curls peeked from under a large white cap, and a large man with no hair save a ring of brown fringe. All his trouble had been for naught.

Lady Whitefield's minion spent the rest of the evening picking bits of potato, onions, and carrots from his coat and eating them. That was likely all he'd have to eat until daylight.

Sarah rose later than usual the next morning, having gotten to bed so late, but then the entire household seemed to have slept longer than was their habit. No doubt even the boys had stayed awake late discussing Sir Evan's heroics and his health. She spent a bit more time on her appearance than usual, making certain her hair was in a neat chignon. The style seemed more appropriate for her role as a widow. Curls would have been nice but without a maid and a curling iron that was out of the question.

On her way to the kitchen she stopped and listened at the parlor door, but not a sound emanated from the room's depths. That was good, since the gentleman could use as much sleep as possible. She made her way to the kitchen and stoked the fire in preparation for breakfast. Within thirty minutes baking cinnamon buns filled the air with a wonderful aroma.

As she cleaned the tabletops, a head appeared at one of the open kitchen windows. "Good morning, Mrs. Ward," Hawks called though the window as he lifted his felt hat from his gray hair. "Sorry I'm late, but Mr. Joiner came by Twin Oaks to ask about Sir

Evan. His lordship's housekeeper sent fresh marmalade for the gentleman, as well."

There was little Sarah could do about those at Longdale being interested in their injured tenant. Yet this sudden flurry of visits worried her. She could only be thankful that the earl was gone on his honeymoon trip, which she hoped would be a long one.

She went and lifted the latch on the rear door. "I don't think you are late. I have heard nothing from Sir Evan's room and I hope he is still asleep."

The valet entered the kitchen, carrying a small portmanteau. He handed the marmalade to the lady, hung his hat on a peg, then excused himself to go and see to his master. Within minutes he returned, asking for water to shave the gentleman.

Pouring hot water into a basin, Sarah inquired, "How is he this morning?"

"Surly as an old bear." He grinned at the expression on her face. "He's never been fit for company before nine even when duty called. Lets me know he's on the mend."

Sarah chuckled. It was hard to imagine the kind gentleman she knew as surly. "What should I prepare for his breakfast?"

Hawks sniffed the air. "Bacon, eggs and he's a fondness for cinnamon rolls, ma'am. As do I."

"Then come and tell me when you are finished, and I shall have his tray prepared."

With a nod of his head, the servant took the basin and left. Sarah worked with an eagerness that surprised her. She wanted to be reassured that all was well with her guest. Then her thoughts returned to the feel of his warm lips on hers and she blushed. She was in no position to be pursing an association with a gentleman with the secrets she possessed. And, after all, neither was Sir Evan. His heart seemed to belong to the undeserving Violet. That is all there was to the matter.

Thirty minutes or more passed before Hawks returned to inform her that the baronet was ready for his breakfast. She poured hot water into the teapot, put a dozen rolls on a plate beside the plate of eggs and bacon, then headed for the parlor, her heart beating at a surprising rate. The servant stood holding the door open for her.

She stepped into the room and halted in surprise. There beside the freshly shaven Sir Evan sat little Luther, his head bent over a checkered board in which a game of draughts was in progress. The gentleman looked up and smiled at her. "Good morning, Mrs. Ward. As you can see I have had an early visitor. He came to inquire about my health, so of course I had to challenge him to a game of some skill."

Sarah's mouth twitched, for even the youngest of children could be taught the simple game, but Luther beamed with pride as he looked shyly through his bangs at Sir Evan.

"Well, the game shall have to wait until after you have both dined. Mr. Hawks, would you remove the draughts board?" Sarah waited for the servant to clear the table, then she placed the tray between the man and child. "Would you prefer milk, Luther?"

The child merely nodded his head. "Then I shall bring you a glass from the kitchen."

Sir Evan noted only one cup. "Won't you join me?"

A frisson of delight raced through her that he'd asked, but she was forced to decline. "The others will be up soon and I must have their breakfasts ready as well."

About to depart, Sarah froze at the sound of the

front knocker. Who could it be? Her gaze moved to the gentleman's face and he appeared to be watching her intently. "Perhaps it is Dr. MacGregor?"

Sir Evan shook his head. "No, he said he was going to visit a friend in Chatford and would not come again until Friday."

Sarah didn't know what to do. What if it were Barlow? Might he have found them?

Once again the knocker rapped sharply. Both men seemed to be staring at her with a questioning look, but despite her best effort she could not make her legs move toward that door. She closed her eyes and prayed for a miracle.

Seven

The clatter of footsteps on the stairs and Jamie's shouted, "I shall see to the door," sent a wave of relief rushing through Sarah. He would turn away any unwanted visitor. She opened her eyes and gazed straight into a pair of questioning emerald orbs. With a wan smile at Sir Evan, she sputtered while she wracked her befuddled brain for an explanation. "It—er—that is I am feeling a bit out of curl this morning."

The strange look never left Sir Evan's face, but Hawks sprang into action. "Allow me to finish preparations for breakfast for the boys. Come, Luther, you can tell me what must be done before the others awaken."

The lad scrambled down from his seat. He grabbed a roll then marched off to the kitchen with Sir Evan's servant. Before Sarah could explain further, the sound of a raised female voice echoed in the hall. She listened intently but it was not a voice with which she was familiar.

Moments later Jamie hurried into the parlor, two females hard upon his heels. "I tried to tell them we are not receiving, Mother—"

A petite, older female with drab brown curls crimped under a black bonnet announced, "Nonsense, my boy. MacGregor told me Sir Evan is here and well on the mend. There is nothing like visitors to hasten one back to the pink of health."

The woman's dove gray morning gown was of the plainest design with only a bit of black frogging to relieve its monotony. Beside her stood a Diamond of the First Water, whose golden blond loveliness was marred only by the petulant set of shapely red lips. Clearly this was mother and daughter, for they each owned the same amber eyes and pointed chins. Yet on the mother the features gave her a sly foxy look, while on the daughter they looked ethereally beautiful.

Sarah could not imagine what had brought them to Wild Rose, certain as she was that Cassandra Ward had never entertained. The time was also well before the proper hour for making such calls. Still, Sarah did her duty and stepped forward. "May I help you, madam?"

The older woman raked Sarah with an assessing gaze, then as an afterthought smiled. "Why, you must be Mrs. Ward. I am Mrs. Henry Newbury." The lady halted on seeing the puzzled look on her hostess's face, she added, "I am the vicar's wife and this is my daughter, Miss Angela Newbury." The girl did a slight curtsy as if they deserved no more, then resumed looking bored and sulky in a pink sprigged muslin gown that complemented her well-rounded figure.

Mrs. Newbury continued. "Likely you will not remember, but I called upon you, my dear, when you first arrived in Shrewsbury. Only your servant told me you were quite unwell." Again the assessing gaze swept Sarah up and down. "I see you are positively blooming. There is nothing like Shropshire air for curing what ails a person I always say." With no sincerity in her voice, the visitor turned to the baronet.

"Sir Evan, I heard the dreadful tale of your ordeal from Dr. MacGregor. Lucky you are to be alive. I felt it my duty to come and welcome you to the neighborhood." Scarcely taking a breath, she continued. "But I see we have interrupted your breakfast. I warned Angela we were early, but she insisted we had been remiss in not calling sooner."

"Do sit down, ladies." Sarah, despite a decided distaste for the woman, gestured to nearby chairs. "May I offer you a bit of refreshment?"

"Tea will be quite enough," Mrs. Newbury spoke as she maneuvered her daughter into the chair closest to the baronet. After a hurried look about, she settled into one nearer the fireplace.

Sarah arched one brow at the gentleman during the ladies settling, noting the obvious action on the part of the mother. The lady's matchmaking seemed to know no bounds. Sir Evan's expression had grown so pained Sarah wondered if his wound was again hurting him. Or was he used to such obvious ploys by marriage-minded mothers?

There was little she could do to protect him from the intrusion, so Sarah moved to the doorway. "I shall only be a moment."

With a sinking heart, Sir Evan watched Mrs. Ward depart. He detested the Mrs. Newburys of the world. They made it their one goal in life to see their children wed to the best matrimonial prospect available, with no regard for love and respect. Violet's mother had been much that kind of woman, and he suspected she'd been behind the girl's defection when the wealthy viscount had arrived in the neighborhood at an opportune time. Had his scars been only the excuse? Then it occurred to him to wonder if he would have truly wanted a female whose affections were so easily swayed by financial considerations? Perhaps instead of the loss of his fiancée, he'd actually had a close escape.

"Tell me, Sir Evan, what brings you to Shropshire?" Mrs. Newbury interrupted his revelation.

About to use the same fabrication he'd invented for his covert mission, he thought better of it and instead said, "I am merely come to see the countryside and recuperate from the war." It would never do to mention historic churches to the vicar's wife or he would have her and her daughter as so-called guides regardless of how little they knew of the buildings.

"Such a pity you were again injured and on Lord Longmire's property." The lady paused a moment, a speculative gleam in her brown eyes. "And did you meet the new earl before he departed on his honeymoon trip? Few in Shrewsbury have had that pleasure, so busy has he been on the estate."

Certain there was a great deal of speculation about Titus in the neighborhood, Sir Evan shrugged. "I engaged my cottage through the steward after the earl departed. I fear I have nothing to say about the young gentleman." There was such a finality in his statement, one could scarcely continue the subject.

A flash of disappointment raced across her face, then Mrs. Newbury looked about the room for a moment as if she were searching for a new topic. "This is quite a fine cottage. I had never been inside it before today."

"I believe that Mrs. Ward and her boys think it so." As the baronet made the remark it suddenly dawned on him that no matter what he discovered about Cassandra Ward's past, he would never help

Titus to force her out. An actress she might have been, but she was no vulgar creature who would embarrass Lady Longmire should they meet. His friend would have to make other arrangements for his mother-in-law. And so Sir Evan would tell his friend when he returned from his wedding trip. Still, it did not lessen his interest in finding the truth about the lady.

The vicar's wife continued to make general conversation, all the while prying into the baronet's situation. He gave little in the way of response, always polite but never surrendering more than was necessary about himself.

Mrs. Newbury, growing uncomfortable with the gentleman's abbreviated answers, looked toward the door. "It is taking Mrs. Ward's servant a long time for that tea."

"Their man is gone to visit his sick father, I believe. The lady is handling things in the kitchen herself."

Mrs. Newbury's eyes widened at such news. "Well, I'm certain that is quite a talent," the lady said with a sniff, "but I am quite unused to having to do such menial jobs, nor would my Angela know one end of a pot from another."

Sir Evan couldn't help but say, "The big hole on top is where the water goes in. It is really quite simple."

Angela snickered and for the first time since the pair had entered the room, he had the heart to pity the girl for having to tolerate such a pushing mother. All that was immediately at an end, however, when Miss Newbury's brow puckered and she asked, "But if her servant is gone, is it proper for you to be staying with her?"

Bright-eyed, Mrs. Newbury eagerly said, "Angela

is correct, sir. I cannot think it the thing to endanger a lady's reputation by lodging here without benefit of her servant. Widowed as she is, Mrs. Ward cannot ruin her chances to make a second advantageous marriage for the sake of the boys. After all she is quite young to be widowed. If you should like I could have my husband's man bring the traveling carriage, and we could transport you in comfort to the vicarage, where you may recover without the least inconvenience. Nothing shabby at the vicarage. I do assure you, sir. You must think of Mrs. Ward's good name."

Sir Evan would far rather be carted off to the gaol than spend time in the Newburys' household. "Thank you, madam. Your offer is too kind, but my own servant, Hawks, is here helping. I cannot think that any gossip would circulate since few even know about me or my forced stay at Wild Rose." He gave her a warning look which dared her to repeat such information.

The door to the parlor opened then and Hawks came in carrying a tray. "Mrs. Ward is with the children in the dining room, sir. She begs you will excuse her and enjoy your refreshments."

Sir Evan spent the next ten minutes fending off more prying questions from his guest and her daughter. At length the lady rose, drawing on her gloves. "Well, Sir Evan, it has been delightful. I do think you should reconsider your position on staying here at the cottage. *I* would never carry tales about such a compromising situation, but these things do have a way of getting about. If you decide you wish to come to us in town, merely send your man and my husband's carriage will be here posthaste."

Thanking the lady, Sir Evan whispered good riddance under his breath as the women finally departed. But he lay back on the daybed and pondered what she'd said. Was he doing damage to Mrs. Ward's reputation? When Hawks returned to the parlor after showing the women out, the baronet put the question to him.

Raising a bushy brow, the valet said, "Well, sir, 'tis neither here nor there as I see it. The doctor has ordered you to stay put for at least a few more days. Can't risk reopening that wound. Don't worry about a bunch of wagging tongues. Mrs. Ward won't care a fig, I assure you."

After his servant left, Sir Evan closed his eyes to rest. The widow was not a social creature who wasted her days on rounds of visits or parties. She would care little about such petty gossip. Still he wouldn't want to inadvertently harm her. He would leave as soon as the doctor declared he might. In the meantime, he remained in a situation to discover what mystery lurked at Wild Rose. The look on her face at the sound of the knocker was unmistakable. Cassandra Ward was terrified of someone.

Over the course of the next several days, the baronet's health improved and something of a routine settled into life at the cottage. Hawks ruled the household with gentle but firm orders. He encouraged the boys to join Sir Evan in the afternoons, always with orders not to stay overlong. The lads loved the time they spent with their injured guest since he would tell them adventurous tales, or they would take turns playing quiet games with him. Mark and Luther played draughts, Alan, Adam, and Peter preferred jackstraws while Ronald and Jamie liked chess and backgammon. Often Hawks would take the younger boys out for a game of tag or cricket, leaving one of the older boys to read the *Morning Post,* which was sent over from Longdale each day by Mr. Joiner. This gave the baronet the opportunity to gently pry with casual questions, but all to no avail. As Sir Evan informed Hawks one afternoon, "These boys would make excellent soldiers. They are as tight-lipped as any exploring officer I ever encountered. I don't think even the French could make them tell a thing about their mother."

The lady of the house proved even more elusive. To Sir Evan's disappointment, he rarely saw her. What bothered him the most was that the more she stayed away from his company, the more he wanted her there to watch the way her eyes would light with laughter or her gentle touch on one of the boys' heads when they sat at her feet. Perhaps he had been right upon first seeing the cottage; it possessed some magical quality that made even the simplest thing enchanting.

Things for Sarah were no easier. She discovered numerous jobs to keep her from the gentleman's presence. Her heart seemed to be betraying her, even knowing there could be nothing between her and the gentleman while the falsehood stood between them. Still, in the evenings she could find no excuse not to join the boys and the gentleman in the parlor. She found herself as intrigued as the others by his travels and experiences in the Peninsula.

On Friday Dr. MacGregor arrived to see the patient. Pleased with Sir Evan's continued recovery, the doctor announced that the gentleman might arise from the daybed.

"Then I must return to Twin Oaks?" Sir Evan

could not hide his disappointment. Despite his continued efforts, he'd learned little.

"Absolutely not." The doctor closed his bag with a snap. "You may move from this parlor to the front one to enjoy the view of the river or to the dining room to join the others at table, but you cannot be jostled about in a carriage. Do not overdo. That wound is healing nicely but cannot be put under any undo stress or it will open again." MacGregor turned to the lady of the house. "Do not allow him to leave too soon, Mrs. Ward, or all your hard work will have been in vain."

The lady smiled at Sir Evan. "Oh, the boys and I shall see that he does not leave until you say the word, Doctor. We know the one thing he fears the most."

Sir Evan's brow rose. "And what is that, madam?"

"Hawks."

The gentleman's eyes twinkled. "To be sure. Such a fearsome fellow."

The servant entered the room in time to hear the remarks, but made no comment, merely harrumphed as he offered the doctor tea, which the man accepted. Knowing that the boys were waiting anxiously to hear the news, Sarah excused herself.

In the rear garden, she informed the brothers that Sir Evan's wound was improving but he would be staying with them for several more days. With shouts of joy the boys returned to their games. After Sarah went back into the kitchen to begin preparations for their evening meal, Jamie, Peter, and Ronald settled on the benches at the rear of the cottage, watching the younger lads play tag.

Jamie, a thoughtful expression on his face, asked, "Have you noticed how Sir Evan looks at our Sarah?"

Peter stopped stacking pebbles into a tower on the bench. "Like she's got a fly on her face or something?"

His eldest brother snorted. "No, silly, like she is a sticky bun and he should like to devour her."

Returning to his pebble stacking, Peter shrugged. "Well, that makes no sense, for then who would make more sticky buns?"

Ronald rolled his eyes. "I think what Jamie is saying is that Sir Evan has fallen in love with Sarah."

Peter stood, angrily knocking all the pebbles back to the ground. "Well, he cannot marry her and take her away, for she's ours." The lad stomped off in a huff through the garden gate into the woods.

Ronald's dark brows drew together. "Do you think she might leave us to marry Sir Evan?"

Jamie shook his head. "No, she has given her word she will stay. But there is another possibility. What think you of Sarah and Sir Evan as our mother *and* father?"

Ronald's eyes widened, then he, too, smiled. "He does seem to like us, too. Would it not be wonderful to be a true family again?"

"Then it's settled. We must do all in our might to encourage them." Jamie crossed his arms and leaned back against the cottage wall as if he'd solved the mysteries of the universe.

"But, Jamie, Sarah is not our real mother. Sooner or later he will have to learn she is not Cassandra Ward and that we have been deceiving Lord Longmire."

Jamie made a dismissive gesture with his hand. "What will that matter? It's not as if he knows the earl. He shan't care a fig. It's her he loves, not a name." At that moment the ball flew at him, and he rose, grabbing it before it hit the wall. He raced off to join the game.

Ronald remained on the bench, lost in thought. He was not so easily convinced that all would be as Jamie planned. While the idea of once again being a family beckoned enticingly, he remembered what his father always said. Gentlemen put a great deal of store in honest dealings. He only hoped his brothers would not be disappointed if Sir Evan left after learning what they had done. No one wanted to be played for a fool.

After nearly a week in the rear parlor, Sir Evan rose, determined to move about to help regain his strength. After being shaved and donning clothes brought from Twin Oaks, he used his valet's shoulder and hobbled into the front parlor, where the large windows opened onto the rose-filled garden as well as the prospect of the River Severn. Within minutes of settling onto a sofa beside the windows, Mrs. Ward arrived with his breakfast.

"Good morning, Sir Evan. You are looking much better." She put the tray on the table beside the gentleman. Hawks departed for some unspecified task. Sir Evan had begun to note that *his* servant had, in fact, become Mrs. Ward's, doing many tasks for the lady. It was strange but in many ways the Ward family seemed to be drawing him and Hawks into their family.

"I am feeling much recovered, madam. You have no need to worry that I shall be imposing on you for much longer, I do assure you." The thought of returning to the small cottage in the woods did little to heighten his pleasure of the day.

The lady shook her head as she poured his tea.

"Do not worry yourself about that, sir. The boys have greatly enjoyed your company."

He couldn't resist the question that leapt into his mind. "And you, Mrs. Ward?"

Her gaze never left her busy hands, but in a soft voice she replied, "I—I have as well." She handed him a cup of tea. Blue and emerald gazes locked. The air almost seemed to shimmer with electricity, then a door slammed somewhere in the cottage, breaking the spell. She returned to putting his plate of buttered eggs, ham, and toast on the table, a pink flush on her cheeks. "Hawks is a great help also."

His gaze lingered on her lovely mouth. He was overwhelmed with an urge to crush her in his arms, to taste those sweet lips. Startled by such a hunger, Sir Evan struggled to gain control of the urge. In a casual tone he was far from feeling, he stirred his tea. "He is the best of fellows in war and in peace."

With a nod of her head, the lady stepped toward the door. Pausing, she inquired, "Is there anything else you need, sir?"

"Thank you, no." He hated to see her go but knew it was for the best. She possessed some magic that drew him like a moth to a flame. He fully understood how Titus's father might have been so intrigued with the lady that he would have acted as he never had before and given her this valuable cottage to use.

When the door closed behind her, Sir Evan shoved the cup and saucer on the table. He ran his hand through his hair, disarraying the neat Brutus style. What was happening to him? He had never been in the petticoat line. Yet he sat here utterly bewitched by a woman with a questionable background. If he didn't recover his strength soon and return to Twin Oaks Cottage he might do something he'd regret. He must never betray his old friend nor take advantage of the lady's hospitality in such a manner. Perhaps it was merely that being somewhat incapacitated made him more vulnerable to her charms.

With new determination to control his emotions, the gentleman finished his breakfast, then sat watching the sunlight dancing on the river, butterflies flitting among the rosebushes, and the occasional carriage rumbling past the small cottage. He tumbled ideas about in his head, looking for a way to help Titus, without harming Cassandra Ward and her children. He knew his friend planned to offer them a cottage elsewhere, but Wild Rose was one of a kind. Likely he was being fanciful, but this building truly seemed to own some mystical quality.

Hawks came to remove the tray. "Do you have need of anything else, sir?"

"Not at the moment." Sir Evan's gaze remained on the scenery.

"Then I'm takin' the lads over to Twin Oaks to help me curry and feed the prads, if you don't object."

The baronet turned to smile at his servant, remembering his own love of horses as a lad. "They shall enjoy that, and I'm certain their mother could use the respite."

"Aye, they're good lads but seven keep one busy." Tray in hand, the servant departed, and soon the house grew strangely still.

Sir Evan would never have thought it, but he'd come to enjoy the sounds of the boys' footsteps, chatter, and laughter. Strange, since he'd fled his own home partly to avoid his niece's children. With a confused shrug, he picked up a book from a nearby table, determined to keep his thoughts away from the beautiful lady of the house.

The gentleman did his best to become engrossed in the exploits of Alexander the Great, but at last he tossed the book aside and stared out at the countryside. It reminded him that his own estate had been left rudderless for too long. Things would be different when he returned home. One thing for certain, he would have to deal with his sister and her domineering ways. She was quite a contrast to the quiet yet efficient Mrs. Ward.

Wanting to put his hostess out of his mind, he rose and limped to a nearby rosewood secretaire, where he found pencil and paper. How better to pass his time than to jot down plans for changes he would make at Beaumont Hall. Returning to his seat, he put everything from his thoughts but work.

Sometime later in the morning a sound drew his attention. He spied Cassandra Ward cutting roses at the far end of the cottage garden. As the sunlight streamed through the trees onto her, she looked a vision in a dark green muslin gown. Her black hair hung loose down her back, kept from her face with a green ribbon. She held a basket of cut roses on her arm and would stop each time she cut a new flower to lift the bloom under her nose and savor the scent. The act was one of such pure enjoyment, Sir Evan wondered how he could live with himself if he betrayed her trust and helped Titus.

Suddenly, to his utter amazement, he watched the lady duck under the overhanging limbs of a nearby rhododendron. He rose from his position, and limped closer to the window to better see. She appeared to be trying to hide as she drew further back into the branches. Was this some game she played with the boys? He waited a moment, expecting to see one of the children come from the rear garden to find her, but instead, he heard the creak of the front gate.

To his astonishment the giant of a man from Shrewsbury stepped through the gate into the garden. What could he be doing here? Surely the man had given up the search for his little girl?

Several sharp raps on the door announced the man's intention to inquire within. When a second set of knocking echoed in the hall, Sir Evan remembered that Hawks and the children were over at Twin Oaks.

Sir Evan limped to the door. Opening the oak portal, he asked, "May I help you?"

The giant's eyes seemed to glitter a moment before he said, "I'm lookin' for Miss Sarah Whiting of Whitefield Manor, sir. Her was washed down the river several weeks ago and rumor says the girl's alive."

Sir Evan's eyes narrowed. The man's story had changed since their first encounter beside the river. "I know of no Miss Whiting."

The giant pulled his hat from his head, his tangled gray hair flying in all directions. He burrowed into the fuzz with a dirty finger to scratch behind his ear. "The chit might be usin' a different name, sir, what with her attic to let and all. I seen her, meself, and know her's alive."

"I do assure you, I have seen no female of questionable sanity." Every instinct told him not to trust the man, who smelled of fir boughs and . . . potatoes.

Tugging the hat back on his pate, the giant shrugged. "Well, her don't look addlebrained. But then often the most dangerous ones don't. Right comely a wench, sir. Hair as black as a raven's wing and eyes bluer than the sky. Twentyish with a shapely build. Looks the angel, but don't be deceived by the girl. Her's a danger and I'm lookin' to take her home where her can be kept safe."

A chill raced down Sir Evan's spine. This hulking gargoyle had just described Cassandra Ward. Yet nothing about her besides her appearance fit what the man claimed. Even as that thought entered his mind, he was aware of the woman hiding in the bushes to his far left. What did this man have to do with her? Is this whom she'd feared all along? Yet how could that be?

"As I said, I know of no such girl." He didn't know why, but he experienced this strange feeling that his hostess knew something about the giant. It would certainly explain her strange reaction in Shrewsbury. "Good day." He closed the door in the man's scowling face.

The baronet limped back to the window and watched the giant of a man lumber back to the gate. After stepping out and closing the wooden entry, he stood and stared at the cottage for a moment, then marched off down the road toward town.

Sir Evan slumped onto the sofa, his mind in turmoil. Earlier, he'd toyed with the idea that Mrs. Ward might be an impostor, but had regarded the notion as absurd. Could his suspicions be true? And if so, where was the real Cassandra Ward? The idea was so fanciful, even now, he couldn't fathom that such a trick could be accomplished. There had to be another explanation.

Some minutes later, the sound of the front door closing drew Sir Evan's attention. He'd left the door to the parlor ajar and he watched Cassandra Ward hesitate a moment, before she put down her basket and entered the room. Or was she Sarah Whiting?

Her hair was mussed and there was a small red scratch on her cheek. Her lovely face was flushed and there was no pretense about her. Yet fear tinged her voice as she asked, "W—what did he say?"

Sir Evan paused a moment, pondering what to do. Would she tell him, or would there only be more subterfuge? He decided to take a gamble. "He said that you are not Cassandra Ward, but a Miss Sarah Whiting."

Her face went deadly pale. She closed her eyes and began to sway. "The worst has happened. W— what ever shall I—I . . ."

Without another word, Mrs. Ward, or was it Miss Whiting, swooned to the carpet in a dead faint.

Barlow watched the quaint cottage from the edge of the trees. He'd recognized the gent the moment the door opened. The giant chuckled, sounding like a low rumble of thunder. It wouldn't be the first time someone underestimated his brains. No matter what the flash cull had said, there was little doubt Miss Sarah was there somewhere, hiding. He found a comfortable spot beneath an old oak and settled down to wait.

The servant didn't have to linger long. Within a matter of minutes, he spotted a dark-haired female slip from the bushes. She paused to look furtively about, then hurried to the front door, and without a knock, dashed inside. So, he'd found her. He straightened and gave a satisfied grunt. The girl was there, but how was he to get her away from the gentry cove what seemed to have her under his protection? He sat some thirty minutes pondering possible plans for luring Sarah away from the cottage, but each time he realized the plot wouldn't work.

The sound of laughter echoed in the wind, distracting Barlow from his mental exertion. Within minutes a small army of boys came frolicking along the road with a squat gray-haired man bringing up the rear. More worrisome, a great hairy dog danced at their heels and Barlow drew back behind a tree, fearful the animal might get his scent.

To Barlow's consternation, the entire lot headed for the cottage, entered the garden, and then went straight inside. The animal paused a moment to sniff at the air, but a soft whistle beckoned him inside and the door soon closed. The man sighed with relief, but wondered how the devil was he going to get the girl out of that crowd?

"Lud!" he muttered. Why should he give himself a headache tryin' and pondering how to get the little jade? All he need do was tell Lady Whitefield where her stepdaughter was hidin'. He'd let her ladyship handle gettin' the girl back. The other matter they would take care of once the chit was safely back at the dower house.

Having settled the problem to his satisfaction, Barlow rose, brushed the leaves off his clothes, and with a jaunty step, headed back toward Montford and a decent meal. Starved he was, but of one thing he was certain: He never wanted to see a potato again.

Eight

Sarah fought back from the darkness that engulfed her. Her eyelids felt too heavy, and the only thing she sensed was a warm feeling of serenity. Disoriented, she couldn't think of anything but feeling safe and protected. Then her memory returned and her eyes flew open.

Sir Evan's face hovered only inches above hers as he held her in his arms. The intense look in his emerald eyes overwhelmed her, making her tremble with some undefined emotion. He smelled of sandalwood, and its masculine essence teased her senses, only adding to her confused thoughts.

"Miss Whiting?" There was a question in his voice that asked about more than her condition.

Closing her eyes, she turned her face away. Shame pushed aside all other sensations. A falsehood stood between them and she was to blame, but there would be no point in continuing her charade. Barlow told him all.

"I *am* Sarah Whiting, sir. Please forgive this masquerade, but there were many reasons and all with the best of intentions."

When he didn't speak, she looked back at him and saw only kindness etched on his scarred face.

"I would never judge you without the entire

story." He looked as if he intended to say more, then seemed to think better of it. Sarah would have sworn it was guilt in the shadows in his eyes, but then perhaps it was only that she was so overset by her own conscience.

"You are very kind."

He looked away, then his brows drew together. "Where is the real Cassandra Ward?"

"I fear she died some months ago, long before I came to the cottage." She repeated what Jamie had told her about life at Wild Rose Cottage. She watched the frown come on the gentleman's face when she mentioned that the boys had been quite alone for over three weeks before her unintentional arrival.

"What can have happened to this Phillips?"

"Jamie swears he is a good and reliable man. It makes me fear for his safety, sir."

A thoughtful look settled on his face. "Then they are alone and penniless in the world without this cottage."

"Not exactly penniless. There is a solicitor from Portsmouth who sends them a quarterly allowance, but even that may stop should he learn of Mrs. Ward's demise." Sarah suddenly realized that she was still in the gentleman's arms. Her cheeks warmed and she shifted her weight in an attempt to sit up. "I am fine, sir. May I stand?"

Without the least embarrassment, the baronet struggled to his feet from the position he'd taken on the floor. Then he took her hand, helping her to her feet. He led her to a green-striped sofa, only releasing his hold once she was settled. She still felt a bit woozy and thanked him.

"Would you like a glass of wine?" He moved toward several decanters that were on a nearby table.

"I am quite recovered, I do assure you." Sarah smiled reassuringly, and he poured a small measure for himself. There could be little doubt that she could trust him and she felt foolish to have let her imagination run wild when they'd first met.

"And can you tell me about this giant of a man who is looking for you?" The gentleman emptied the glass then limped back to where she was seated. A sense of elation raced through her that she no longer had to carry the burden of their secret by herself.

Then her thoughts focused on his question and her sense of well-being fled. Her gaze dropped to her hands as a wave of fear coursed through her. "His name is Barlow. He is my stepmother's groom. I do not know for certain, but I believe she had him throw me in the river to drown me."

Sir Evan put his hands behind his back, a frown marring his brow. "What exactly happened?"

She kept her tale brief. Starting with the trip to Montford and the new dress, she told of the flooded river and Barlow carrying her to the middle of the bridge. "Then he stepped to the edge and tossed me into the water."

"And you are certain that he did not slip or lose his grip?" Doubt tinged his voice.

Sarah knew her tale sounded incredible. Her thoughts returned to that moment of fear on the bridge. Had it been an accident? Had she once again let her imagination get the better of her? "I— I'm not certain, but I would swear that he intended to throw me in the water."

The gentleman grew quiet, a thoughtful expression on his face. Fear and shame warred in Sarah's breast. How could he trust her word after she'd impersonated the boys' mother? To him she must appear some foolish chit of a girl spinning tales like the ones in those Gothic novels that some of the girls at Miss Parson's so loved to read.

He startled her when he asked, "Was there a great deal of acrimony between you and the lady?"

Now for the first time since she'd been pulled from the river, Sarah began to doubt all her conclusions. "Well, no, in truth, she's spent the better part of the last seven years since my father died ignoring me." Had her dislike of Lucinda clouded her judgment? Perhaps Barlow was insane and had acted on his own. She shuddered as the groom's grotesque face flashed in her mind.

The gentleman again interrupted her musing. "Was there something about your life that had altered recently? Something new or unusual?" Sir Evan's gaze never left her face, but she could see the doubt on his.

"Only that my father's aunt left me a modest legacy." Then she hastened to add, "But I shall not have access to the funds until I'm five-and-twenty, which is almost six years in the future."

Sir Evan, at first doubtful of this fantastic tale of intrigue, saw the truth at once. "But that factor would have no bearing after your demise, Miss Whiting. The funds would go immediately to your next of kin. Have you any relatives besides this step-mother?"

Sarah Whiting shook her head, but before she could explain more about her circumstances, the front door opened. The Ward children entered the front hall, along with Hawks, and after a quick whistle by Peter, Percy bounded in to sniff at the baronet's boots. On seeing the lady and gentleman in the front parlor, the boys poured into the room, full of chatter about Sir Evan's grays and their trip to Twin Oaks.

The baronet's mind was a jumble of startling new details. Everything about his mission to Wild Rose was changed. But he needed time to sort out what to do. Time to determine when he would tell Miss Whiting the truth about why he was in Shropshire.

The boys began to ask for something to tide them over until supper. Sarah, as he now knew her to be, rose with a hesitant look in his direction.

He gave her a reassuring smile. "We shall speak later. The boys need nourishment after their visit to Twin Oaks and all their hard work." Hawks, unaware of the undercurrents between his master and the lady of the house, began to usher the lads into the hall with promises of milk and biscuits. Sir Evan put his hand on the lady's shoulder before she departed. "Have no fear. For the present all is well. This Barlow knows nothing about your presence here. I promise we shall keep you safe from harm."

The trusting look in those blue eyes almost undid him. A desire to crush her to him and kiss away her fears rose in him; to reassure her that no one would harm her or the boys whom she loved. But he stayed the impulse and allowed her to walk out of the room. His secrets were not yet revealed, and his uncertainty about her feelings held his wishes in check. After she closed the door, he limped to the windows to organize his thoughts. His gaze raked the surrounding terrain as if he were on sentry. Danger was out there and he must not forget that fact. This Barlow had left, but it was clear he hadn't given up looking for his prey.

Strange, but his entire acquaintance with Sarah Whiting was one large pretense on both their parts. Would there be any hope for some kind of a future with this woman? In his heart he held hope that she would forgive him for his own deceptions.

His energy spent, he collapsed on the sofa and began to ponder Miss Whiting's revelations. What was he going to do? With their mother dead, the boys no longer had the right to live at Wild Rose. Titus would be well within his rights to send them away, not that he thought that his friend would put them into the street. But he was certain to take possession of the cottage. Sarah Whiting had no connection to the boys other than affection. She was merely an innocent victim of her own—

Suddenly he sat up. It had not occurred to him until that moment that he had been living under the same roof with a gently bred female without a chaperon, not a widow and her children. Miss Whiting might be too innocent to realize what that meant, but he was not. Without further delay, he rose and limped from the room. Of this he had no doubts, he must return to Twin Oaks Cottage this very day.

"Alive!" shrieked Lady Whitefield amidst the shattering of crockery. Her teacup disintegrated into pieces as it struck the dining room floor creating a dark stain on the Oriental rug. "But you promised she was dead."

Barlow shifted nervously before his mistress even as he eyed the slices of roast beef and ham in a tray on the sideboard. "Survived her dunk in the water, her did. Livin' near Shrewsbury with some gentry cove and a passel of lads."

A dark red stain rose on the dowager's lovely cheeks as she began to pace back and forth at the far end of the room. "This won't do, you fool. Cornell, no doubt, has set his own men to look for the girl." She turned to stare at Barlow. "If he finds her first . . . there shall be hell to pay."

The giant shrugged, never taking his gaze from the abundance of food before him. "Scarcely had enough blunt to buy me a crust of bread, much less the entry to hell, my lady."

Ignoring the man's inane remark, the lady paused. "Residing with some man, you say?"

The groom bobbed his head. "Gentleman, he were, but says he didn't know Miss Sarah. I reckon her's usin' another name."

"Very likely." Lady Whitefield walked to the window, her back to her servant. The man, noting her distraction, filched a slice of roast beef, jamming it whole into his mouth. His cheeks bulged, giving his troll-like countenance the strangely benevolent appearance of a doting grandfather, but her ladyship took no note as she turned back to him. The lady's face was a mask of cunning.

"That shall play very well into my new plan. The girl would be ruined if it were revealed she has been sharing this man's home. I shall go and fetch her back home. We must give the servants the day off, then only you and I shall know she still lives. You can show me this cottage, can you not?"

Unable to speak with his mouth full, Barlow bobbed his head. "Um, hum."

The dowager looked about as if she suddenly realized her meal had been disrupted. She stepped to the sideboard and rang the bell for the maid to come and clean up the mess, then settled into her chair. "That will be all, Barlow. I shall not need you until the morning." She paused a moment, staring at the man. "You do not look yourself. What have you been doing since you left?"

The groom hung his head and mumbled a few unintelligible words.

"Oh, never mind. You have found her and that is what is important. Go now and I shall see you in the morning. I will inform Cook you may have some reward. Wait outside the kitchen door."

Barlow's face contorted into what might have been a smile as he hurried from the dining room. He went out and round the dowager house, munching happily on the beef. In his opinion, the encounter had gone surprisingly well. They would go to get the chit and be done with this dark business.

He settled on the stairs to await his reward. There was still the matter of what they would do with Miss Sarah, but Barlow was still too hungry to put his thoughts to such. After all, there was always the river if nothing else came to him.

The door to the kitchen opened and a scrawny maid edged out. "H—her ladyship told us to give this here to ye. It was all what was left."

The frightened girl held out a tray covered with a cloth. No sooner had Barlow risen and taken his promised treat than the door slammed shut in his face. So ravenous was he that he settled right on the stairs to eat. Whisking away the white linen, he revealed a beef bone, nearly stripped of meat, a few peas, and to the man's disgust, a large bowl of boiled potatoes.

"Leaving?" Sarah looked from the baronet to his servant as a tremor of fear shot through her. She and the boys would be alone to face Barlow if he returned. "But Dr. MacGregor said you were not to set foot from the cottage."

She watched a look pass between the two men,

then Sir Evan stepped forward and took her hand. He cleared his throat as if what he had to say was difficult. "Miss Whiting, we are not abandoning you. Hawks and I shall be close at hand. You need only send one of the boys and we shall be here. Perhaps you do not realize it would do your reputation no good should anyone reveal that I have been staying under this roof with you without a chaperon."

"Chaperon?" Sarah gave a mirthless laugh. "Sir, little about my life for the past several weeks would find approval with Society, but I care not. Do not risk your health over such a trivial matter."

His hand came up as if he might touch her cheek, then halted, going instead to adjust his cravat. "You are young, my dear, and do not fully understand. What happens here in this cottage could affect the rest of your life. I could never live with myself, if I were responsible for causing you the least harm."

Sarah could see he was resolute and there would be no changing his mind. The strange urge to cry welled up inside her, but she turned away so that the gentleman and his servant would not see her distress. She'd faced taking care of the boys alone before Sir Evan came to the cottage, and she would do so again. There was one other matter she had to broach. Gaining control of her emotions, she turned to face the men.

"Sir, much depends on what happens next. Our very safety is in your hands. Will you keep our secret?"

A strange look passed over Sir Evan's face, almost as if some great pain had struck him, but he never wavered or groaned. At last he quietly said, "I shall never do anything that would harm you or the children." Without further comment, he turned and departed the room with an awkward gait, instructing his servant to join him.

Hawks smiled. "Have no fear, miss. We'll be close at hand. Sir Evan and me faced many a column of Frenchies. He told me of this stepmother, and we ain't afraid of no Lady of Quality and her groom, be he giant or no." The servant then hurried from the room.

Moving to the window, she stared out with unseeing eyes. She could hear the boys calling sad goodbyes, then the sounds of a carriage moving away at a slow but steady pace. She closed her eyes and prayed. Sir Evan might think he would be able to do his best to stop Lucinda and Barlow, but Sarah was not so convinced.

Why did she feel so abandoned? She hardly knew the baronet, but she could no longer deny that the gentleman stirred deep feelings within her. Then she remembered the look that had passed between Sir Evan and Hawks. Did they see her as little more than a foolish schoolgirl who didn't understand what she was doing? But she did; she merely didn't care about the strictures of London Society. There was also the woman named Violet that Sir Evan had called for her in his fevered mutterings. Sarah knew she'd been beyond foolish to put her hopes in a man whose heart belonged to another.

"Sarah," Jamie called from the door, interrupting her painful musings.

She grabbed the window frame for strength. Sir Evan was gone, even if it was only a short distance away. It would be best to put him from her mind. She turned and smiled at the eldest of the Wards. "Is everything well?"

The boy shrugged. "I sent the others out into the garden." He stepped into the parlor, a ripple of worry marring his young brow. "What is going to happen now that Sir Evan has departed?"

"Why, we shall go on as we did before he came. Can I rely on you once again?"

Jamie's head bobbed vigorously. "As far as anyone knows, save Sir Evan and Hawks, you are still our ailing mother." His frown returned. "Will they keep our secret?"

Sarah fussed with her apron, hoping the boy wouldn't see the tears which again threatened. "Don't worry about Sir Evan or Hawks." It dawned on her that he had only promised to do nothing to harm them, not to keep their secret. She pushed the thought aside. She'd scarcely been on her own again five minutes and her imagination was once again in full bloom.

The boy grinned. "I knew he was a great gun."

Determined to keep her wits and appear normal, she asked, "Did you now? Well, if my memory serves, you were the one saying we should not see him."

Jamie gave a dismissive gesture with his hand. "That was before we knew him and he saved Luther." He grew quiet a moment, then looked at her sideways. "You do like him, do you not?"

She more than liked him, but she was not going to torture herself. "We have no time to waste worrying about Sir Evan, dear boy. He is only next door, and I am sure we shall see him again." That thought made her feel better. She ruffled Jamie's hair. "I must begin supper or we shall have an angry mob on our hands come six o'clock."

Jamie laughed and followed Sarah to the kitchen. Work would help her forget those emerald eyes, and there was always plenty to do at Wild Rose.

* * *

Hawks strode round the end of Twin Oaks Cottage to find Sir Evan seated on a bench beside the front door, just where he'd left him before taking the carriage and horses to the rear shed. "Are you well, sir?"

Sir Evan nodded. "A bit tired, but I shall survive." He fell into silence once again, leaving his servant to reopen the cottage and prepare an evening meal. As Hawks lit a fire, the former batman wondered what the baronet intended to do about the lads next door. He'd grown uncommonly fond of those boys and hated to think what would happen to them even in the best of orphanages. He grabbed the poker and shoved the kindling closer to the fire, which flamed up with a crackle.

"Hawks."

The servant looked up to see Sir Evan standing in the door. "Is there somethin' you need, sir?"

The gentleman limped into the cottage, easing down into one of the straight-backed chairs at the rough-hewn table. "I want you to return to Beaumont Hall in the morning."

Hawks frowned. "Beggin' your pardon, sir, but you can't be left unattended. What if you was to take a turn for the worst and me not here to see to you?"

Sir Evan made a dismissive gesture with his hand. "I am recovered enough to take care of myself for the few days it will take for you to do what I wish."

The servant put down the poker as the flames grew. "What is it you're wantin, sir?"

"Go to Appleby, my solicitor in Lyme Regis, and have him find me a suitable cottage near Beaumont Hall for Miss Whiting and the Wards. I shall send a letter ordering him to follow your instructions."

A grin lit the servant's face. "Capital, sir. I knew you wouldn't let no namby-pamby vicar take them lads to some orphanage."

Sir Evan gazed into the fire thoughtfully. "This all depends on me convincing Miss Whiting that I meant the boys no harm."

"You think the lady's goin' to be piqued at learnin' you was here on Lord Longmire's business?" Hawks puckered his lips a moment then said, "Well, sir, it ain't like she and the lads didn't tell Mr. Joiner a great bouncer, and so I'll remind her if she becomes missish."

"Oh, I could never see Sarah as missish. I don't know many young females who could have endured what she did in the river, then step right in and take over when the boys needed her. No, I was thinking more that she will feel I betrayed them."

Hawks brows shot up but he didn't say a word. Sarah was it now? So that was how the wind was blowing. The servant turned so his master wouldn't see the grin that split his face. "I shouldn't worry myself on that one too much. She's a right sensible lady." He moved to stoke the fire, his mind racing.

He peered over his shoulder at the baronet, who sat gazing at the flames, lost in thought. Hawks had an idea.

"Sir, I've got to fetch some more wood."

The gentleman nodded absent-mindedly as Hawks exited through the back. No sooner had the door closed than the man broke into a full run, heading straight into the woods. He followed the path to Wild Rose and was gasping for breath by the time he reached the fence that enclosed the Wards' rear garden.

"Miss Whiting," he called to the open kitchen windows, where he could hear the clatter of crockery.

The lady appeared in the open door, wiping her hands on a cloth. "Mr. Hawks, is something wrong?"

"Not a thing, ma'am. I just come to ask a favor."

Exhausted from his dash through the woods, he didn't cross into the garden. Instead, he waited for her to come to him, which she did.

"Anything." She smiled and Hawks knew that he was doing the right thing.

"Got to go to Dorsetshire in the mornin', miss."

A tiny crinkle appeared on the lady's brow. "Surely Sir Evan is not going to make such a journey so soon?"

"Not he, ma'am. I'm goin' to handle some business for him. That's why I come to ask a favor. He tells me he can take care of himself, but bread and cheese ain't a proper meal for a man recovering his health. I was hopin' you might take him somethin' hot and delicious while I'm not there to see to his needs."

There was a moment's hesitation, then she nodded. "I shall certainly see that he eats properly while you are away."

"Ma'am, you're a regular trump." He looked a bit startled, then added, "If one can say that about a lady."

Sarah laughed. "I am not offended. I shall bring him his dinner and see how he is doing."

Hawks tugged at his hat. "Thank you. I must get back and see to him. Good day to you, ma'am, and don't forget, if you need anything send one of the lads for the baronet. And don't worry, he is any man's equal with a pistol even injured." The servant turned and hurried back along the path to Twin Oaks, leaving Sarah with mixed emotions. Perhaps it would be best that she not see Sir Evan again for the sake of her own heart, but somehow she couldn't resist the opportunity to be near him, perhaps for the last time.

Nine

Hawks cinched the girth tighter one last time, causing the horse to shift restlessly. "I don't feel right about takin' one of the carriage horses, sir. What if you need to go to town while I'm gone? I'm certain Lord Longmire's steward would allow me to ride one of the home farm's mares that ain't breedin'." The servant lingered on the ground, fussing with the leather saddle straps, not wanting to leave. He'd dawdled much of the day away doing unnecessary tasks, hoping the baronet would change his mind about sending him to Dorsetshire.

Sir Evan, standing in the doorway of the cottage, laughed. "I am much improved today, but still in no condition to be driving to town. You need have no worry about that. There is bread, butter, cheese, and ale. I shall be quite cosy here until you return. Should I have need of anything unusual, I am certain that Titus would have no objection to my asking at the manor house."

"Shall I fetch more wood for the fireplace?" Hawks began to retie the reins to the fencepost.

"There is a small tower beside the fireplace, and I am not expecting a snowstorm this late in May." A twinkle glinted in the gentleman's eyes.

"I really should bring more water from the well." The man started toward the gate.

"Nonsense! I have more than enough since I won't be entertaining." The gentleman crossed his arms, his tone full of finality. No matter what excuse his man had to delay, Sir Evan would parry with a reasonable response to counter his argument.

Hawks shrugged, then turned back to the horse and mounted. With a final grin, he announced, "Oh, but you shall have a visitor. I forgot to mention that Miss Whiting is coming to bring you somethin' for to eat. That shall be a treat."

"What do you mean?" Sir Evan straightened, anticipation evident on his face.

"I went over yesterday and told her I'd be gone for several days. The lady promised to make sure you were properly fed."

"That wasn't necessary." The gentleman's words were stern, but a smile played at the corner of his mouth and his eyes took on a faraway quality as if he were imagining the lady already by his side.

"Didn't want her to think we'd abandoned her, should she or the lads learn I'd gone and you not up to your full fightin' weight, so to speak. Which reminds me, a pistol is primed and ready beside your bed should the need arise." The valet turned the horse round, then paused to look over his shoulder. "If you'll pardon my sayin' so, it might be a good time to clear the air of any further secrets, sir, let her know what's what with his lordship." The man gently nudged the horse's ribs.

"So, it might," Sir Evan said thoughtfully. Realizing his servant was finally leaving, the gentleman waved as Hawks cantered down the lane back to the road south. As the sounds of the horse died away, Sir Evan knew that Hawks was correct. But how best to broach the subject of Titus to Sarah and explain the whole truth about his real reason for coming to Wild Rose? Perhaps he should wait until he'd heard from Hawks that a new place was ready and waiting for Sarah and the boys before he revealed everything. It would take some persuading, but even if she didn't forgive him, she wouldn't be foolish enough to turn down a secure home for the boys.

The distant drumming of a horse's hooves echoed through the trees, and the baronet listened intently, wondering if the rider was coming to Twin Oaks or to Wild Rose. An urge to get his pistol raced through him as he remembered the giant at the cottage, then it was evident that the hoofbeats were coming up his lane. Had Hawks once again found some paltry excuse to keep from his task? If so, the gentleman meant to give his servant a rare trimming and send him on his way. He wasn't helpless and could manage a few days without the man.

As the sound drew nearer, Sir Evan realized it wasn't a single animal but two horses cantering along in near perfect cadence. He peered down his lane and caught sight of two riders on the narrow overgrown path. A bright blue feather spiraled above a fashionable velvet cap of one and with a sinking feeling, Sir Evan recognized his visitors.

He stepped to the gate to greet Lord and Lady Longmire, newly returned from their brief honeymoon trip. As Titus called a hello, Sir Evan debated how much or how little he should tell his friend about Sarah and the boys' deception.

A tray sat on the table covered and ready to be carried to Twin Oaks Cottage. Beneath the linen lay a small roast hen, creamed potatoes, as well as cooked cabbage, along with a loaf of bread and a pear tart. Sarah nibbled nervously at her lip, pondering if she should send Jamie with the food or take it herself. The others would want to go along with their older brother, which might be inconvenient, so she decided to deliver the gentleman's dinner herself. She wanted to make certain he was well.

She opened the oven one last time to inspect the poppy seed cakes she'd put in a few minutes earlier. They would need another thirty minutes. She looked at the clock on the mantelpiece. She could deliver the meal before it got cold and return in time to take their favorite treat from the oven.

The boys were in the rear parlor, listening to a story that Ronald was reading as they did often, and wouldn't miss her. She picked up the gentleman's dinner and exited the rear of Wild Rose. The path through the woods was easily discernible and she made her way to the back of Sir Evan's cottage. The place seemed deserted, but she could see he'd left the windows open, taking advantage of the late afternoon's warmth. The new yellow curtains fluttering at the windows seemed an odd touch for a man's abode, and she was curious who had hung them. As she approached the cottage, she heard voices in the air. Puzzled, Sarah wondered if Hawks had delayed his journey to Dorsetshire. He'd been concerned about leaving the baronet unattended during his recovery.

She hesitated a moment when she discovered the rear door ajar and debated whether to put the tray on the bench beside the door or to go inside. A gust of breeze pushed at the oak door and with a loud squeak, it opened completely. She could see that the cottage was empty. Afraid to leave the tray where it might not be found, she stepped into the cool depths of the cottage. No one was in the small room off the main room, but voices could be heard coming from the front of the cottage. She put the tray on the table and stepped to the window to peer out. To her surprise she saw Sir Evan greeting a fashionable lady and gentleman on horseback.

Sarah's heart froze when Sir Evan's words drifted to her. "Marriage seems to be agreeing with you, Lady Longmire. I believe you more lovely than you were when you married my old friend."

The gentleman beside her ladyship said, "What's this, Beau? I leave you to investigate the Wards at Wild Rose and I return to find you a glib-tongued rogue. Be careful, Georgina, it is the quiet ones you have to watch out for."

Lord and Lady Longmire! Sarah closed her eyes and leaned back against the cottage wall in horror and realization. There could be little doubt that Sir Evan was a close friend of the very man that she and the boys feared most. The man who could take away their very home. Why, the baronet had even gone to the earl's wedding. Worse, he'd been sent to spy upon them. A small sob escaped Sarah's lips as a complete sense of betrayal washed over her.

The pain within her heart seemed to grow so strong she was afraid she might faint there inside the cottage. Blindly she fled toward the rear door, barely able to see the opening through her unshed tears. Outside, she hoped she might breathe without the tightness gripping her chest, but as she rushed back into the woods, she knew no amount of fresh air would take away her pain.

Her thoughts were in such turmoil that she'd reached the back gate of Wild Rose before she was able to gather her wits enough to fathom that she couldn't let the boys know what danger lay ahead for them, not until she had a plan. Entering the garden, she went to the small bench under the trees and collapsed. She fought back the tears as an even more startling realization settled in her heart. She'd fallen in love with Sir Evan—a man who was not what he'd seemed to be. Why, Sir Evan Beaumont was a fraud. He'd come on the Earl of Longmire's behalf, and there could be little doubt what that gentleman wanted—to have the boys out of this valuable cottage. She couldn't be certain that anything the baronet had told them was true.

Hands tightening into fists, Sarah straightened as her gaze swept the beautiful little cottage. This was not about her or having foolishly fallen in love. No purpose could be served if she wept and lamented *her* pain. Her first thoughts must be for the boys. Those dear, sweet boys who'd not only lost their mother but would soon lose their home. There was little doubt they would be forced to leave, but where would they go? Tamping down her dejection, Sarah had no clue where they might turn, but whatever happened she would never let the boys be sent to the workhouse as long as she had breath.

As the smoke from the kitchen chimney wafted on the breeze, she gasped in dismay, then dashed into the house. Pulling the cooked cakes from the oven, she was relieved to see they weren't burnt. She pushed the trays onto the table, taking little note of the wonderful aroma filling the kitchen. Staring at the golden brown poppy seed cakes, she decided if worse came to worse she could cook for funds to support them.

The thought of money brought her solicitor to mind. What had happened to Mr. Cornell? Why had he not come, or at the very least written to acknowledge her letter? Time had run out and she wouldn't be able to wait any longer. Sir Evan was speaking with Lord Longmire even now. No doubt in the morning Mr. Joiner would be knocking on the door to inform them that they must leave within the hour. Would he bring the local magistrate? After all, they had pretended that Mrs. Ward was still alive.

A tremor went through her. She wouldn't be able to do anything if she were in the gaol. Perhaps they should simply leave early, before the steward had the opportunity to confront them. They could use what money Jamie had left to take the stagecoach out of Shrewsbury, but to where? London? The very thought sent another shiver down her spine. She would have to figure out the best place for them to go. Wherever they went, she would tell the boys the truth after dinner this evening. With a heavy heart, she set about preparing their final meal at Wild Rose.

"Titus, my love, what can your steward have been thinking to put Sir Evan in this dreadful little cottage?" Lady Longmire took her first look at Twin Oaks after the baronet's greeting. On dismounting with her husband's assistance, her gaze swept the former tenant cottage, and the deficiencies were obvious. She was so intent on taking in every detail that needed work she did not see the knowing look that passed between the gentlemen.

"My dear, old campaigners never worry about such things as accommodations. Why during the war while we were in the mountains, a cottage this well made would have been a veritable palace, I declare." The gentleman eyed his property with pride. "My men are doing all the repairs, are they not?"

Sir Evan nodded. "They are. Besides, 'twas I who

requested this cottage. It's nice and quiet here down near the river."

Doubt clouded the lady's gray eyes. "I cannot believe that you prefer to stay here now that Titus and I have returned. Do come up to the Hall with us. My mother and sisters shall arrive from London tomorrow. They should like nothing more than to entertain a handsome gentleman."

"My dear Georgina." Longmire patted his wife's hand and saved Sir Evan from having to explain. "Beau requested to stay here, which means he cannot want to be up at Longdale with a bunch of chattering females. There are some times in life when a gentleman wants nothing more than to be alone." He gave his wife a piercing look.

Her ladyship's cheeks flushed pink at the memory of what her husband had told her of his friend being jilted only months earlier. "I do apologize, sir. I didn't think . . . that is—" She looked desperately about for another topic, then her gaze fell on a nearby clearing in the trees. "Such pretty wildflowers. I shall go and pick some for my sisters. They prefer them to the hothouse variety." Lady Longmire hurried away without a backward glance.

Sir Evan waited until the lady was out of earshot. "Your wife need have no fears that I am suffering any lingering pangs about Violet. I have spared hardly a thought about the lady in the past few weeks, and those have been mostly ones of relief."

The earl eyed his friend thoughtfully. "I must say you are looking much more like the man I knew in the Peninsula rather than the poor wretch I visited down in Dorsetshire." Longmire shot a hurried glance in his wife's direction then lowered his voice. "What have you learned about this creature and her passel of brats?"

Sir Evan gritted his teeth. A spark of anger burned deep within his chest at his friend's deriding tone. Then he realized Titus was speaking of a woman Sir Evan had never met. He knew Sarah Whiting, not Cassandra Ward. The memory of those blue eyes as she'd pleaded with him to protect their secret flashed in his mind. He came to a decision.

"Give me a week, Titus. I should have everything regarding Wild Rose wrapped up to your satisfaction by then."

The earl's pale brows drew together. "Can you tell me nothing?"

"Not at present. Truth be told I know little, but I promise to tell you everything I know at the end of the week."

His lordship grunted with dissatisfaction. "I still don't understand what this woman's hold over my father was."

"Nor do I. I'm not even certain Mrs. Ward was an actress. I only know that she came from Portsmouth and has a solicitor there. But that is neither here nor there."

"A solicitor, perhaps—" A glint appeared in Longmire's eyes.

"That doesn't matter. Only be assured that I shall take care of matters, and you will have your cottage back." The baronet's tone was sharp. He wanted Sarah safely settled in Dorsetshire before he told Titus everything.

But the earl was not to be fobbed off. His gaze roved thoughtfully over Sir Evan's face. "Beau, you haven't fallen for this creature as well? I know from Joiner that you stayed there a few days after some accident involving a boar."

The question took Sir Evan by surprise as well as the answer which came to him in an instant. He did love Sarah Whiting, with all his being, but would she ever forgive him for having deceived her and spied on her? He experienced a surge of fear the likes of which he'd never known, even when facing the French. He just might lose the woman he loved because he'd tried to help a friend. Seeing Titus's wary eyes, he said, "Don't be ridiculous. I am not in love with Cassandra Ward." That he could state unequivocally. "I just need a week and then I am certain you will have your cottage."

Thankfully, Lady Longmire returned at that moment, keeping the earl from asking more questions, which Sir Evan could see he had by the worried expression on his face. Her ladyship, recovered from what she preceived to be her faux pas earlier, invited the baronet to dine later in the week. Sir Evan promised he would come, and the worry lines relaxed from Titus's countenance.

"Promise you will. And have an explanation for everything."

"I promise."

Lord and Lady Longmire remounted and bid Sir Evan good day. The gentleman watched the pair until they were out of sight, then feeling restless he moved to sit on the bench beside the front door, his thoughts in disarray. Would he be able to make Sarah understand? Would she forgive him? He was so lost in contemplation and doubt that it was almost dark when he entered the cottage to light candles and discovered the tray.

Sarah or one of the boys had been there! When? A cold fear gripped his heart. Had they seen Titus and realized the truth? Without a thought to his injured leg, he knew he had to go to Wild Rose at once to explain everything. He set out limping through the woods with one thought replaying in his mind. He couldn't lose Sarah; he loved her too much.

Lucinda fingered the small green bottle she'd gotten from the apothecary in Montford. The man had been most sympathetic, having heard of the loss of her beloved stepchild and was eager to give her a potion to help her sleep. He'd warned her to be careful with the elixir, but after all, what did it matter if she administered too much to the girl? A smile tilted her mouth as she slipped the bottle back into her reticule.

She looked across the aisle of the carriage to see Barlow watching her carefully. She never should have allowed the oaf to ride inside with her, for he took up so much space, but it would never do for Sarah to see the man before it was time to take her from the cottage where she was hiding.

"How much farther?"

The hulking groom peered out the windows. "We'll reach the place 'afore dark."

The lady nodded her head, then said, "Stay in the coach until I send for you. Are you certain this driver you hired will keep his mouth shut?"

A frightening grin lit the man's hideous face. "Him's more scared of me than any beadle of the law."

Lucinda didn't doubt that. Some thirty minutes later the carriage drew to a halt and the door opened. The white-faced driver, who scarcely looked old enough to shave, glanced at Barlow and cringed, then he stuttered out, "T—this here's the p—place what Barlow described, my lady."

The dowager stepped to the ground. She surveyed the small cottage in the distance, and her brows rose in surprise. Even in the fading light she could see the place was quite lovely. Perhaps once she was again in funds she would find a similar place near Dorchester, where she'd grown up. Then she discarded the idea. If she went home it would only be to live in one of the finest houses in the country. No more poky little cottages for her.

"I won't be long," Lady Whitefield announced as she went toward Wild Rose with a determined step.

"It's mine; I found it in the garden," Adam cried as he and Peter tugged on the same tin soldier. The disturbance flared up after dinner when all the Ward boys were settled in the rear parlor. Jamie grinned at Ronald across the chess table and shrugged his shoulders, as if to say Not again, and moved his bishop. Mark and Luther stopped playing jackstraws to watch, but offered no opinion as to whose toy soldier it might be. Alan yawned, then after a quick glance at the bickering pair, returned to his book.

"You know I put my regiment in the window this morning to dry after I painted them. It's mine." Peter jerked at the toy, but his younger brother held on tightly.

"I tell you it's—"

"Boys, what is this?" Sarah entered the room carrying a tray with their evening tea, putting an end to the dispute.

"Is that all for us?" Peter asked as he eyed the tray, losing interest in the tin soldier which he released. The toy disappeared into his brother's pocket.

Putting the tray on the table, Sarah began pouring glasses of milk for the younger ones. Several plates were squeezed onto the tray, each containing a large stack of food. One held cinnamon buns, one poppy seed cakes, one macaroons, and the largest one was full of pear tarts.

"Are we having a party?" Mark's eyes grew round at the sight of so many wonderful things to eat.

Sarah couldn't explain to them she'd spent the remainder of the afternoon baking to relieve her anger at Sir Evan and her frustration over not knowing how to find funds to take care of the boys once they left from Wild Rose. She'd finally come to the conclusion she could go to Lady Rose Dennison. Surely her friend would be able to help her find work in York, even if it were only cooking for some widower. To the Wards she merely said, "Sit down, boys. I want to have a very nice tea this evening." It took several minutes for everyone to find a seat and Percy, fascinated with the tray of food, had to be shooed to the fireplace rug.

Sarah looked at all the eager faces and a pang touched her heart. In a few short weeks she'd come to love them all. This was going to be the hardest thing she'd ever done, for she knew they loved Wild Rose. It was the last place they had shared with their mother.

Before Sarah could speak, Jamie asked, "Can we go over to help Mr. Hawks with the horses in the morning?"

"No!" Sarah practically shouted the words, then calming herself, she added, "Mr. Hawks has returned to Dorsetshire and won't be there."

"Is Sir Evan gone as well?" Ronald asked, then he cast a strange look at Jamie.

She struggled to hold back the tears at the gentleman's name. How could he have come to them under false pretenses like some sneak thief in the night? Her own little deception paled in comparison in her mind. "Can we not have our tea in peace? We will discuss such matters after we have eaten."

Jamie, sensing Sarah's heightened emotions, rose and passed out the plates. "We can do whatever you wish." The boys filled their plates and oohed and ahed over the pastries and cakes.

"Tonight will be our last—" She halted and listened a moment. "Did you hear something?" Strange but she thought she heard the creaking of the front door.

"It was likely just Percy," Peter said before taking a large bite from his cinnamon roll.

Sarah listened for several moments more, then, thinking it her imagination playing tricks on her, she once again started. "As I was about to explain, tonight will be our last—"

The door to the parlor swung open and there, to Sarah's horror, stood her stepmother, looking even more beautiful than Sarah remembered.

"Why, my dear child, I have found you at last. You cannot know what a great deal of trouble we have gone to locate you." Lucinda grinned a grin that could charm the birds from the trees, but her eyes glittered coldly.

Ten

Sarah started from her chair, tumbling macaroons, tarts, and plate to the rug. Percy pounced
upon the windfall, paying not the least attention to
the visitor. "Mother!"

Lucinda strolled into the room as if she'd been
invited to tea. The black gown she'd donned in
mourning for the benefit of the neighborhood only
added to her ethereal quality, making her porcelain
skin glow and her golden curls more striking. "What
a quaint place, my dear. Quite charming, in fact."
She looked at all the boys, who had risen and
flanked Sarah like a protective shield. "My, but some
poor creature has been kept busy by her husband."

A flush of anger warmed Sarah's cheeks. "What
do you want here?"

The dowager's eyes widened as she drew off her
kid gloves. "But my dear, can you doubt that I want
to take you home where you belong? After all, I am
your guardian."

Sarah's chin rose defiantly. "I am not the same
fool who came back from school, madam."

A cunning look settled in the lady's blue eyes.
"Do you truly wish to discuss family matters in front
of the children?"

There could be little doubt in Sarah's mind that

the argument with her stepmother would become heated. "Come, children." She shepherded the boys toward the door.

"Oh, my dear," the dowager called to her departing stepdaughter, "would you bring another cup for tea? This looks quite delightful."

Sarah turned to see Lucinda standing beside the tea table, smiling as if there were nothing out of the ordinary about her visit. Once the boys were in the hall and the door closed, they crowded round Sarah, fear on their faces. Jamie acted as their spokesman. "Are you leaving us?"

"I promised I would not."

Ronald said, "But since she is your mother, must you not do as she wishes?"

"She is only my stepmother and I shall do as I wish, which is to stay and take care of you all." She smiled at the boys. Despite her own fears, she knew she must reassure them first. "Don't worry, I shall make her understand she no longer has any power over me. Peter, will you go and bring a cup and saucer?" As the lad dashed to the kitchen, she said, "Stay here and be quiet. I shall go back and . . . explain to her that I cannot leave you nor do I have any wish to return to living under her roof."

Jamie took her hand, his face looking far older than his twelve years as he said, "If you need us, you must only call out and we shall be there in the wink of an eye."

She patted his hand. "I shall."

When Peter returned with the cup and saucer, Sarah made a gesture of silence with her finger, then slipped back into the parlor. The door had barely clicked shut when Jamie turned to Ronald. "I don't like this lady and I think she means to make Sarah go with her. I am going to Twin Oaks to summon

Sir Evan. He will know what to do. Listen and if she calls go to her at once."

Ronald nodded his head, even as his eyes widened at the possibility. Jamie hurried down the hall and out the rear door.

"What shall we do if she calls?" Ronald asked the others.

Peter balled his hands into fists and held them up in front of him like a fighter. "We go to her rescue."

"But Sarah said the lady is her mama," Alan argued. "We cannot go in there and mill down a female. It ain't proper."

"She is her *stepmama,*" Peter said, with an arched brow. "You have read enough stories to know they are always the wicked ones."

All the boys nodded their heads, except Ronald. "That is utter nonsense, Peter. Sarah has been like our stepmother these three weeks, and she is wonderful." But no one seemed to be listening, for they all had moved to press their ears to the door when voices sounded in the parlor. Without further protest, he joined them.

Inside the parlor, Sarah discovered her stepmother seated and nibbling on a bit of poppy seed cake. She came to the table and poured the lady a cup of tea. She handed the cup to Lucinda and was surprised that her hand did not shake. "I am not going back to Montford with you."

"My dear, do sit down and finish your tea. We can discuss this like adults." Lucinda picked up Sarah's cup and handed it to her.

Hesitating a moment, Sarah took the cup, taking a gulp to steady her nerves. It had grown cold and seemed bitter, as if she'd brewed it too long. As she settled in the chair opposite her stepmother, she noted the lady watching her intently. There was no use delaying what she had to say. "I know that Barlow tried to get rid of me at the river and you—"

Lucinda's tingling laughter filled the room. "You always did have a fantastic imagination, child. Barlow slipped and dropped you, that is all. Why, he has been beside himself with worry and grief, combing the banks of the Severn for weeks. You can ask anyone. But that is not the least important nor is it what I want to discuss. There are far more urgent matters. Where is that man?"

Sarah's brows drew together. "What man?"

"The one you have been living with here at the cottage. You must know that your reputation is quite ruined. There can be no suggestion of a Season for you now."

A strange feeling seeped into Sarah. She knew she should be angry with her stepmother, but suddenly she seemed too tired to worry about such things. "You . . . are mistaken. There is no one—" Sarah's eyes closed and the cup and saucer slipped from her hand and crashed to the floor into pieces. Unconscious, she, too, slid to the rug with a thump.

Lucinda rose, a smile lighting her face. That had been excessively easy. She put her cup on the table, but before she could step to the window and signal Barlow, the parlor door flew open. There was a moment of stunned silence as the brothers spied Sarah crumpled on the parlor floor.

"Get out you little beasts. This is none of your affair. Sarah is my step—" But she was unable to finish what she intended to say, for a swarm of angry boys rushed at her, all shouting and throwing whatever they could find at hand. Even the dog joined in the assault, barking and snarling at the woman.

To Lucinda's dismay everything the lads hurled at her seemed to stick to her hair, her face, and her gown. Then she realized she was being pelted with the remains of their tea—sticky buns and pear tarts. "Stop that, you horrid little monsters." But her protests only seemed to spur the boys' fury. She tried to back away from the onslaught, but slipped on a bit of pear tart and tumbled to the rug. "Stop!" she shrieked.

A male voice ended her misery. "That will be enough, boys. I do believe she is waving the white flag."

A cold chill clutched Sir Evan's heart at the sight of Sarah on the floor. He went straight to her and took her in his arms. "What did you do to her, madam? If she dies, I swear I shall hang you myself from one of the trees outside."

Lucinda scrapped icing from her eyes to see a gentleman staring at her with such steely dislike she drew back and stuttered, "S—she is not dead, only drugged with laudanum. I have to take her home, and the silly chit is being disagreeable."

"Hear me well!" The gentleman's tone was cold. "Sarah is not going with you now or ever. I know what you had your man do, and don't try to deny your part in Sarah's being thrown in the river. If ever again you or your man come near her, I shall see that you are both arrested and put in the gaol."

"Who are you to be speaking to me that way?" Lucinda blustered. She rose and bits of pastry fell to the floor, but many more remained stuck to her. "I am Lady Whitefield and Sarah is my ward. You have ruined my stepdaughter and so I shall tell—"

Sir Evan stepped toward the dowager, Sarah

clutched firmly in his arms. "Never speak Sarah's name again, madam. She is my future wife, and I shall very much take it amiss if I should learn that you have so much as breathed a word about her. I believe the magistrate in Montford, is it, would find what we have to say very interesting."

"You have no proof and cannot—" a defeated Lucinda whined.

"Boys, escort Lady Whitefield from the cottage. You have my permission to set the dog upon her if she is not fleet with her departure." With that Sir Evan turned and took Sarah out of the parlor.

"Don't touch me, you little beasts." Lucinda drew back as the brothers began to tug at her gown, drawing her into the hall. One boy picked up her gloves and shoved them at her. About to reach for them, she took one look at the dog's bared sharp teeth and hurried from the cottage.

Within five minutes a very subdued dowager stepped out of the darkness beside her carriage. "Open the door, you oaf, and unshutter the carriage lantern, we are going home."

Barlow scrambled out, and did as he was ordered. His eyes widened when the golden rays from the large lantern revealed the sight of his mistress. "What happened, my lady?"

"Oh, do be quiet and take me home." She climbed into the carriage and slumped onto the squabs. "It is finished. I shall have to go back and marry that dreadful Lord Hargrove."

Barlow took off his hat and scratched at his head after he climbed in opposite her. "Ain't Sarah comin' home? Ain't we goin' to—"

"Don't you ever say that dreadful girl's name again." Lucinda sniffed and reached for a handkerchief, but her hand came away with a glob of icing.

The groom nodded his head, but he was puzzled about what had happened in the cottage. He scooped a spot off her ladyship's gown and sniffed. It smelled quite flavorful. He tasted it and gave a delighted hum. "Pear tart." Once again he plucked a titbit from the gown, "Sticky buns." As he reached for a third morsel, Lucinda grabbed his arm.

"If you take one more bite, *I* shall see you dance at the end of a rope."

Barlow sat back, folding his arms over his barrel chest. Strange, but he couldn't make the lady understand he didn't know how to dance. Quality, why, their brain boxes weren't no better than his.

Sir Evan leaned over the bed and gently patted Sarah's hand but got no response. Looking over at Ronald who stood on the opposite side of the four-poster, he asked, "How much longer do you think she will sleep?" It was strange to be asking a child's opinion, but Jamie swore the boy knew almost as much about medical matters as some doctors. It had been over two hours since Lady Whitefield had fled and he was starting to worry that the potion had been more dangerous than Sarah's stepmother had led him to believe. They had listened to her heart several times and it continued to beat in a steady rhythm.

"It's difficult to say, sir, not knowing how much she drank." Ronald looked at Jamie. "Do we have any coffee? I have read a strong brew will wake—"

A noise echoed in the hallway.

Jamie moved to the open door and peered out. "It sounds like someone is trying to come in through the kitchen door."

Sir Evan moved to stand beside the boy, peering

into the dimly lit hall. "Are all the younger boys abed?"

Jamie nodded. "I made certain not ten minutes ago. Percy's upstairs as well."

Sir Evan's face hardened. Had Lady Whitefield sent Barlow back to take Sarah against her will? "Have you a weapon, lad?"

"Aye, my father's." Jamie went to a chest of drawers on the far wall of his mother's room. "Sarah keeps it here." He took out a key and unlocked the upper drawer of the cabinet.

The baronet pulled open the rosewood drawer and found an ancient dueling pistol atop some linens. He quickly inspected the pan and discovered, to his surprise, it was primed and loaded. He couldn't say she wasn't a sensible girl. "Stay here."

He stepped into the hall and moved stealthily toward the kitchen door, but he'd only gone a few feet when a gaunt man with a battered black felt hat staggered into the hall and nearly collapsed against the wall after a single step. He looked as if he were in his cups, his gait was so unsteady. Sir Evan leveled the pistol at the man. "Halt! What are you doing here?"

"Who *are* ye?" the old man asked, staggering back at the sight of the weapon.

From the bedchamber doorway Jamie cried, "Philly!" The Ward brothers rushed into the hall, throwing their arms around their old servant, almost knocking him off his feet. It was evident to Sir Evan that there was a great deal of affection between the servant and the children as the old man folded them into his frail arms.

"Steady there, lads. Me pins ain't in the best of shape." After a quick hug he gripped the door frame, unable to stand without wavering. Fatigue was etched in his face as he looked back at the baronet.

Jamie leaned back to stare at the older man. "Where have you been? We've been so worried."

Phillips eyed the pistol that remained trained on him. "Ye can stow yer barkin' iron, sir. I ain't no thief, just Mrs. Ward's servant what had an untimely encounter with a team of runaway prads what knocked me senseless."

Sir Evan tucked the pistol in the edge of his breeches, then stepped forward to help the man to a chair, as he looked as if he might collapse at any moment. "You have been injured all this time that the boys have been looking for you?"

The old man allowed them to help him settle before he explained. "Aye, and not just injured but unconscious for near a fortnight in the attics of the Bristled Pig in Shrewsbury, so they told me. No one knew me name so they couldn't tell the lads I didn't desert 'em. When I come to, couldn't even tell 'm who I was." He pulled off his hat to reveal a deep red scar at the edge of his graying brown hair. His chin was scraped with a heavy aberration that looked like it might be permanently discolored. "Scrambled me brains right proper, it did. Then out of the blue this mornin', I was sittin' in front of the stables at the inn when this gent introduces his companion to a friend as his ward and it was like water rushin' into a rain barrel. Everythin' came back. I knew I had to come see how the lads was gettin' on."

Jamie looked at Sir Evan and shifted, uneasily not wanting to blurt out the truth in front of him. "We've handled things very well."

The old man leaned toward Jamie even as he eyed

Sir Evan. "It seems ye've got a bit to tell me about, lad."

"Well, er, that is . . ." Jamie shifted uneasily, shoving his hands in his pockets.

Sir Evan relieved his discomfort. "I know about your mother's death and that you rescued Sarah from the river."

Jamie's eyes widened. "But, how? Sarah swore she wouldn't tell."

"She didn't. It was a groom of Lady Whitefield's who told me who Miss Whiting was. After that she didn't have any choice but to explain the rest." Sir Evan wasn't ready to admit his duplicity to the boys at the moment. They were likely to toss him from the house before he could plead his case with Sarah.

Phillips issued a great sigh. "Well, lads it seems our game is up now that they've winkled the truth out about your mother. Mayhap the earl will let us stay until I'm back on me pens proper, then we'll go to me brother's in Norfolk."

"That won't be necessary, Phillips. Once Miss Whiting and I sort out our differences, we shall take the boys to Dorsetshire." The baronet couldn't help but smile at the look of delight on the boys' faces. "I intend to make the lady my wife, if she'll have me."

"I told you," Jamie bragged to his brother. "Shall we go up and tell the others?" The two boys scampered down the hall and up the stairs.

"Like I said earlier, who are ye, sir?" Phillips gazed warily at the stranger, not as easily mollified by matters.

"Sir Evan Beaumont of Beaumont Hall, Dorsetshire." Sir Evan turned his head at that moment, listening for what he thought was a groan coming from the room where Sarah lay sleeping.

"And what right have ye to be sayin' what happens to these lads?"

He looked back at the servant. "None whatsoever, but I will do as Sarah decides." Almost certain that the lady was coming to, he said, "We shall speak about the boys later, have no fear on that head."

The gentleman strode back into the bedchamber, leaving Phillips scratching his head. "And just who the blazes is this Sarah to be decidin' what happens to the captain's lads is what I want to know?" The old servant leaned back again the chair, realizing he was too tired to pursue the matter that night. He'd just rest there awhile before heading upstairs.

A wave of nausea rushed through Sarah. What was wrong with her? She lifted a hand to her head, which ached, and realized that a ribbon was twined in her hair. She never went to bed with ribbons. With great effort she opened her eyes to find herself in her bedroom. The room was surprisingly well lit but empty; the door to the hall stood open. How had she come to be in bed, fully dressed?

Lucinda!

Sarah sat up and the room spun. She closed her eyes for a moment, groaning as the wave of nausea peaked, then ebbed. At last she was able to open her eyes. Her last memory was of being in the parlor, having tea with her stepmother. The tea must have been drugged, but why had Lucinda not spirited her away?

Before Sarah could sort her confused thoughts, Sir Evan entered her room. He came straight to her. "You are awake, my dear. How do you feel?"

Elation at his concern raced through her, then her memory returned. He was Lord Longmire's friend. The baronet had come to spy on them and had kept the truth from them. "What are you doing here, sir?" She drew back as he reached for her hand.

"My dear Sarah, you must listen to me."

"You have betrayed us." Angry tears sprang to her eyes. Fighting to regain her composure, she peered past him, thinking to see the earl. All she saw was the empty hallway. "Where are the boys? What have you done with them?"

"Put them to bed. It's late." A wry smile lit his face.

She brushed at the tears. "Then I want you to go."

"I won't go until you hear me out. You owe me that, Sarah. You and the boys are not untarnished in the charade of identities."

The look in his eye was so determined there was no point in arguing and she couldn't deny her own duplicity. "Very well, have your say, but it won't change anything. You are—"

Sir Evan sat beside her, taking her in his arms he kissed her soundly, stopping whatever she'd been about to say. His warm lips pushed all thoughts from her mind. Every sense she owned seemed to tingle and she relaxed into his embrace, wanting nothing more than for the moment to never end. What harm could one last kiss do?

He released her, then gave her a gentle shake. "Now, listen to me, Sarah. I have not told Longmire anything about you. Do you think I would betray the woman I love?"

She blinked as she stared into his emerald eyes. The kiss had sent her wits into complete disorder. Gathering her reason, she hoarsely said, "But you are his friend, are you not?"

"Titus saved my life, in more ways than one." He reached up and brushed a dark curl from her cheek, then his hand traced the line of her jaw. "That is why I came, to repay that debt. But it wasn't to take Wild Rose away from the boys and their mother. He wanted to know what hold Cassandra Ward had on his father which made the old man give this place to a complete stranger. I won't deny he wants the cottage, but he would have honored his father's wishes and provided a suitable home for them."

Breathless at his touch, she nibbled at her lip to give herself time to think. He loved her, but there was still the matter of the boys. "Do you intend to tell Lord Longmire Mrs. Ward is dead?"

He captured her chin. "Sarah, this masquerade is at an end. Tell me what you know about the lady."

"I don't know why the old earl gave her the house, nor do the boys. Jamie said he'd never seen his lordship until he arrived suddenly after their father died."

The gentleman rose and walked to the fireplace, then looked back at Sarah. "Their father? Was Cassandra Ward not an actress?"

From the doorway, the old man angrily announced, "She weren't no Bird of Paradise, sir. Right and proper buckled to Captain Ward her was."

Sir Evan grinned at the expression on Sarah's face. "Pray allow me to present you to the missing Phillips. Philly, this is Miss Sarah Whiting, daughter of the late Baron Whitefield, as Jamie has explained to me."

Philly looked from Sarah to Sir Evan. "Right pleased to make both your acquaintances, ma'am, sir, but can you tell me how it comes that ye are here livin' with the lads?"

The clock on the mantelpiece chimed the midnight hour. Sir Evan shook his head. "It quite late, Philly. We shall explain everything in the morning. Where do you sleep?"

The old man motioned upstairs. "In the attic, sir."

"Do you need help upstairs?"

"I walked the entire way from Shrewsbury, sir. I reckon I can go a few more steps without help." With that the old man disappeared toward the stairs.

Sir Evan turned back to Sarah. He folded his arms across his chest. "It is the moment of truth, my dear. I love you. I want you to marry me and bring the boys to Beaumont Hall to live." He paused a moment, unable to read the expression on her face. In a soft voice he added, "But if you do not wish to be my wife, I shall still provide a place for you and the boys on my estate."

Despite this being everything she could wish for, still Sarah hesitated, as her gaze searched his face. "I—I do love you, but what about Violet?"

"Violet! Where did you hear about her? If Hawks has been telling tales, I—"

"You called for her when you were ill with fever. I thought, er, well you spoke of her as if you loved her." Sarah plucked at the blanket that covered her, fearful of what he would say.

Sir Evan returned to her side her and took her face in his hands. "It wasn't until I fell in love with you that I truly understood what love was. She was my fiancée until I returned scarred and crippled from the war." He held up the hand that still had not fully returned to normal. He gave a laugh that held little bitterness. "The lady jilted me for a handsome viscount." His voice held not pain, only a matter-of-fact tone.

Sarah, appalled that a lady could behave in such a manner to a man she loved, traced a finger along one of the scars that lined his cheek. "Lines of bravery there for all the world to admire."

Sir Evan smiled and kissed Sarah. As his passion grew, he broke the connection, moving back to the fireplace to put some distance between himself and the lady he desired.

"I can only say that Violet was a foolish young soldier's fancy of what a proper wife should be. Since I came to Shropshire, I am thankful every day that I escaped such a marriage." He turned to face her, a smile on his face. "And speaking of marriage, will you be my wife?"

Sarah drew the blanket aside, and slipped from the bed to join him at the fireplace, looking up into his eyes. "Are you certain you want a bride who comes with seven eager lads?"

"Miss Whiting, I would take you with thrice as many lads." He took her in his arms and kissed her until she couldn't breathe.

At last he released her, taking a step back. In a hoarse voice, he announced, "I'd better return to Twin Oaks before things get out of hand, my love."

Sarah's cheeks warmed when she realized his touch had lit a flame within her which could easily get out of control. "Perhaps that is best."

"I shall return first thing in the morning to help you explain to Phillips and to help prepare for the move." He kissed her lips, then both her hands before he strode from the room. In a matter of minutes she heard the kitchen door bang shut.

Sir Evan loved her. He wanted the boys as well. She walked to the window and looked out at the moonlit garden. She would miss Wild Rose Cottage, but everything had changed. They wouldn't have to search for a place to stay. Longmire was likely not the villain they'd thought him, but he had a right to his cottage since Cassandra Ward was dead.

She suddenly wondered why the cottage had been given to the widow. Would they ever know the truth? With a sigh, she began to get ready for bed. Hopefully Phillips would be able to tell them everything in the morning.

Sarah pulled scones from the oven the following morning, then spied Philly at the door as she slid the hot tray onto the table. "Good morning, Phillips. Did you sleep well back in your own bed?"

"Miss Whiting, ye don't need to be in here workin' like that now I'm home." The old man looked around the kitchen. "By Jove, I ain't never seen the place lookin' this clean, ma'am, nor the rest of the cottage for that matter."

She smiled. "Thank you, but you know the boys helped."

His brows rose. "Ye ain't jesting? The lads cleanin'?"

"Well, it took a bit of effort, and occasionally one must redo a task after the little ones have finished, but for the most part, they have been wonderful helpers." She gestured for the old man to take a seat in one of the chairs put against the wall out of the way. "You need time to recover from your accident. We can still manage quite well until you are ready to resume your duties."

"It just don't seem proper for me to be sittin' while a baron's daughter is doing the work, miss."

Sarah laughed. "That is nonsense. I am not some

delicate flower, Phillips. Do sit down and let me pour you a cup of tea." When he hesitated still, she added, "The scones are always best warm."

"Right you are, miss." He moved a chair to the kitchen table, settling down to watch as she skillfully poured hot water into the teapot. "But, Miss Whiting, what puzzles me is how ye and the gentleman come to be here at the cottage?"

Sarah took two teacups from the cupboard and returned to the table. "If you don't object, I shall join you while you eat and explain this entire muddle. I can assure you that it has been quite a mix-up of hidden identities and crossed purposes."

"Why, I'd be honored, miss." Philly's faded brown eyes twinkled as the lady moved a second chair to the table to sit opposite him. "I should guess it shall be quite a tale."

"There are times when I can hardly believe it myself." Sarah poured out tea, then began. She and Phillips were still at the table some thirty minutes later when Sir Evan knocked at the rear door.

On entering the room, his gaze locked with Sarah's and her cheeks warmed even as her heart leapt with joy. He squeezed her hands but didn't embarrass her by kissing her in front of Phillips. "Are the boys not awake yet?"

The old servant shook his head. "It was a rather late night for the lads, what with all the excitement with Miss Whiting's stepmother. Then Ronald and Jamie woke the others to tell 'em I was back. They were still up chatterin' when I passed their room so I had to threaten them with my cookin' unless they got to bed." He gave a laugh. "That scared 'em right and tight."

Sir Evan laughed. "If Miss Whiting will allow me a cup of tea and a scone, I shall answer any questions you may have, Phillips." Sir Evan moved to the cupboard and retrieved a cup and saucer and joined them after he brought a third chair from the dining room.

The old servant waited quietly until the gentleman had had his breakfast, then he said, "Miss Whiting done told me how you both came to be here. I've thanked her for all she's done and I'd like to thank you. I've no objections to your takin' the lads with ye to yer estate, but"—the old man's gaze dropped to the table—"I reckon what I was wonderin' is, have you a position for me, sir? I been with Miss Cassie since she married the capt'n."

The baronet put down his half-eaten scone. "I wouldn't think of taking the boys and not taking you, Phillips. Beaumont is a large estate and there are plenty of positions. You may have your pick. You don't even need to decide what you want until we get settled. From that limp I saw last night it appears to me as if you could use a bit more recovery time."

Philly smiled and nodded. "You and the lady are a regular bang-up pair, sir. I don't know how I can repay ye for what ye've done, nay, what ye are doin' for us all."

A thoughtful expression settled on Sir Evan's face. "Perhaps you can if I may ask you one question?"

The servant's brows rose. "Fire away, sir."

"Do you know why the late Lord Longmire gave this cottage to Mrs. Ward?"

A knowing look settled on the old man's face. "That I do, sir, but it came as a bit of a shock to Miss Cassandra, I can tell you." He looked at Sarah, then leaned toward the baronet and in a lower tone announced, "It seems she was the gentleman's natural daughter. His lordship got regular reports on her from a solicitor in Portsmouth. When he heard that Capt'n Ward's ship sank and that the missus was ailin', he came down and offered her Wild Rose."

"Mrs. Ward never knew of the circumstances of her birth?"

"Not until the earl come and told her. She thought herself the daughter of a farmer and his wife. Seems the girl's mother died in childbirth and the lady's sister took her in and raised her as her own since she had no children. Best I can tell, sir, the old earl truly did love Miss Cassandra's mama but he already had a wife."

A frantic knocking sounded at the front door, surprising them all. Sir Evan looked at Sarah, whose face reflected her fears. He covered her hand. "Do not worry, my dear, I shall handle our visitor."

He rose and made his way to the oak portal. Sarah and Phillips waited at the rear of the hallway in the shadows.

On opening the door, an old gentleman dressed in a neat but subdued black coat and breeches stood coughing into his handkerchief. It took him several moments to recover his breath and uncover his face. "Pardon me, but I have come to see Miss Sarah Whiting, sir."

"Mr. Cornell!" Sarah called with delight as she made her way to where the gentleman stood. "I have been so worried. Why did you not write?"

"Child"—he took her hands, giving them a fatherly pat—"you cannot know how delighted I was to receive your letter yesterday. Your stepmother had come and told me some Banbury tale of you being dead, so you can imagine my elation at learning it was all a hum."

"I don't want to think of that wretched woman and her horrid groom, but how is it you only received my letter yesterday? I posted it almost two weeks ago." Sarah drew back in surprise.

"Unfortunately, my secretary kept it from me while I was ailing. A congestion of the lungs after a simple wetting." A rueful smile lit his face. "Not but what I'd have been able to understand your message what with my fever and all. Perhaps he did do the best thing, but all that matters is that I am here now to take you to London. We shall find you a chaperon and a house and you won't ever have to go back to Montford." The solicitor then noted the gentleman, who'd been standing quietly behind Sarah shaking his head. "Who are you, sir?"

The baronet smiled when Sarah blushed and stuttered, "F-forgive my rudeness. Sir Evan, allow me to present my solicitor, Mr. Albert Cornell. Sir Evan Beaumont of Beaumont Hall, Dorsetshire."

After shaking hands with the older gentleman, Sir Evan said, "I think there has been a change in plans since Miss Whiting wrote you, sir. She has consented to be my bride."

The old man frowned as he watched the man put a possessive hand on the girl's shoulder. "Sarah, I would speak with you in private for a moment."

At that moment all seven of the Ward boys trooped down the stairs. Sir Evan smiled, seeing that Sarah was torn between reassuring her worried solicitor and taking care of what she deemed to be her charges. "Take Mr. Cornell into the parlor. Philly and I shall see to the lads. Come along to the kitchen, boys. Miss Whiting has business to handle."

The Ward brothers eyed the lawyer with curiosity, but their stomachs overrode any other thoughts. At the gentleman's urging, they followed the baronet down the hall while Sarah led Mr. Cornell into the front parlor.

The door had no sooner closed than the solicitor said, "My dear, since you have no father I feel that I must act in his stead. I hope you have not accepted this gentleman's proposal merely as a means to take care of yourself and to get away from your stepmother. Your Aunt Phoebe suspected what Lady Whitefield was. She authorized me to draw on the funds should you have need earlier than your twenty-fifth birthday."

Sarah took the gentleman's hands. "It is not like that, sir. I love Sir Evan."

"But, child, to marry a man with so many children, why—"

She laughed. "These are not his children. Well, I guess you could say they are mine."

The gentleman's eyes widened. "Now, that I know to be untrue. You would have still been in the schoolroom when most of them were born."

She lifted her hands. "Only in a manner of speaking. Do be seated and I shall tell you how I came to be here."

They settled on the sofa and Sarah told him everything. It took the better part of half an hour. Near the end of her tale a knock sounded at the door and Sir Evan entered. He glanced warily at the solicitor, whose disapproval had been evident at the front door.

The old gentleman rose and extended his hands. "Forgive my delayed felicitations, sir, but I had to make certain Miss Whiting was making her choice for the right reasons."

As the solicitor watched Sarah and the baronet look into each other's eyes, all doubts were removed by the passion, which seemed almost palpable between them. He smiled, and asked, "Is there anything I can do to help either of you to prepare for this union?"

Sir Evan drew his gaze from Sarah, wishing the gentleman were elsewhere so he could kiss his fiancée. "If you should like to help us arrange transporting seven children, an injured servant, and a great hairy dog to Dorsetshire I should be forever in your debt."

"Well, I was thinking more in the way of legal matters, but I should be delighted." The solicitor walked out of the parlor, opened the front door and shouted, "Frederic, come here. I have a task that will make up for your keeping Miss Whiting's letter from me."

As he waited for his clerk to climb down from the carriage, Mr. Cornell peeked back into the parlor to see Miss Whiting locked in a passionate embrace with Sir Evan. A smile lit the old gentleman's face. He would no longer have to worry about Miss Phoebe's niece. Sarah would be well taken care of by a man who appeared to adore her. What more could a female want?

Epilogue

A caravan of two traveling carriages and a wagon loaded with furniture arrived in front of Beaumont Hall one week later. Mrs. Sorley peered out the front window, wondering who could be visiting without an invitation. Likely it was merely travelers who'd mistaken their way. Jarvis would soon have them set right and gone.

She returned to her chair and picked up the book she'd been enjoying before being disturbed. She was in no mood for guests for the next year, after spending three weeks with her own daughter and grandchildren. Her nerves were quite shattered by the children's great noise and messy clutter. She'd been as pleased about their departure as she had been to see them arrive.

The sounds of chatter in the hall soon disturbed the lady. She looked up from her book, wondering what Jarvis could be thinking to have allowed them access to the house. When the noise grew louder, Mrs. Sorley slammed the book closed and rose, determined to go do what the butler had failed to do, rid the house of these importuning travelers.

She entered the hallway, then checked at the sight that met her eyes. Sir Evan's man Hawks was surrounded by seven lads, a young female, and a battered old servant who looked as if he'd been used as the ball in a cricket game. A great hairy dog bounded over to her, to sniff at her shoes, causing her to draw back. The valet was laughing at something the female was saying, but the smile dropped from his face when he spied her face.

"What is the meaning of this, Hawks?" She'd been looking for a way to get rid of Evan's former batman. He might have been suitable during the throes of war, but he was hardly a proper valet for a gentleman and she hoped this was her opportunity. "Who are these people and why have you brought them here? Where is my brother?"

"Sir Evan shall be here—"

Sir Evan stepped into the great hall at that moment. "Ah, Aggie, I am glad you are here. Allow me to present you to my fiancée, Miss Sarah Whiting." He stepped up and put his arm round the girl, whose cheeks grew quite pink even as she looked up at Sir Evan like a lovesick calf.

The baronet's sister uttered a soft gasp when she thought her brother might forget himself and actually kiss the chit before them all, but he straightened and said, "And these are the Ward brothers, who shall be living with us. I think for the time being they can all be put in the nursery. Sarah can decide about sleeping arrangements later. Phillips will stay with them there until a proper nurse can be engaged and he is feeling more himself."

Mrs. Sorley's eyes nearly bulged at the announcement. Through stiff lips, she said, "Jarvis see to Sir Evan's wishes. Put Miss Whiting in the Willow Room."

The baronet kissed Sarah's hand. "You shall want to rest and change before we dine."

Sarah hesitated a moment, but the dislike on her

future sister-in-law's face was so evident, she raised her chin. "I shall see that the boys are properly settled first."

The young lady followed the butler, Phillips, and the boys up the stairs.

They were barely out of sight before Mrs. Sorley exploded. "What have you been about? Who is this creature? And these children? I begin to think you have become unhinged from your experiences in the war, sir."

"Be careful, sister. Sarah is my future wife. Never again refer to her as a creature if you wish to remain in my home." The flinty glint in the baronet's eyes was one Mrs. Sorley had never before seen.

She hesitated a moment, knowing she must be careful, but her ire was too great to contain for long. "F—forgive me, I am merely overset at the suddenness of your arrival with a . . . a fiancée. You can have scarcely known her above three weeks. Are these children hers?"

"Time is irrelevant. I knew Violet most of my life, Aggie, and still I didn't know her at all. Of one thing I'm certain, Sarah truly loves me and that is what matters. As to the boys, they saved Sarah's life and in many ways she saved theirs. They own a bond which I would never wish to break. They are orphans, so they shall stay and grow up here at Beaumont."

There was a great deal more he could tell his sister about the brothers but the baronet didn't go into the details of his meeting with Titus and the news imparted regarding Mrs. Ward and her sire. As Sir Evan expected, his friend had offered to make proper arrangements for the boys but the baronet had refused, saying Sarah wouldn't be parted from them. The earl had generously promised to set up trust funds for each, a gesture that many of his station would have failed to do. He'd even come over to meet the boys, and promised to visit at Beaumont Hall in the fall.

"Stay!" Mrs. Sorley interrupted Sir Evan's musings. "But you cannot abide children. You left to avoid my grandchildren."

Sir Evan shrugged. "It would appear it is only unruly children I could not abide. I have an affection for these boys."

Mrs. Sorley began to pace back and forth in front of her brother. She was furious. After all she had done for him after their father died, this was how she was to be repaid. Pushed aside for some slip of a girl to run the family home. Even worse, to have her peace and quiet disturbed on a daily basis by a passel of brats who belonged to who knew who. She simply wouldn't tolerate such. She halted, a determined jut to her chin. "A wife! I think you are being a fool to marry someone you hardly know. Her, no doubt I can learn to tolerate, but there is this matter of a houseful of orphans I find even more outrageous. I will not suffer a bunch of noisy boys running about breaking my beautiful—"

"*You* will not suffer? Madam, need I remind you whose house this is?"

Mrs. Sorley put her arms akimbo and defiantly played her last card. "I warn you, Evan, I shall not stay under this roof with those boys."

Sir Evan's eyes narrowed slightly. "Are you saying it's either you or the boys?"

A defiant grin stretched her mouth. "You take my meaning exactly. It is your sister or those nobodies."

The baronet drew his hands behind him, staring at Agnes thoughtfully. At last, he uttered a sigh of regret. "You handled the estate better than most men after I returned from the war and briefly fell into a brandy bottle to relieve my sorrows. I greatly appreciate your hard work, despite some questionable decisions regarding my cattle. It makes it all the more difficult for me to say that I regret that you have made such a choice now. I shall miss you."

With that the gentleman walked upstairs, leaving his sister with her mouth gaped open in utter shock.

Some two hours later Sarah arrived at the head of the staircase, stopping to gaze about the great hall. She had fallen in love with the house the moment she'd seen it from the carriage window. The boys had decided that the beautiful old Tudor house must have a ghost, but Sir Evan declared it was vastly lacking in spectral residents.

Taking in the lovely tapestries on the walls, Sarah found it difficult to believe that she would soon be mistress of such a large establishment. Then she remembered the unwelcoming Mrs. Sorley and wondered if Sir Evan's domineering sister would easily relinquish the reins.

The baronet entered the great hall from a door and looked up to see her on the landing. "You are enchanting, my dear." He extended a hand to her.

Sarah knew the pale green silk gown he helped her pick out in London fitted perfectly. It was certainly a vast improvement over Cassandra Ward's ill-fitting wardrobe, which she'd packed and ordered Hawks to distribute to the poor. She hurried down the stairs and shivered as the gentleman gave her a lingering kiss on the back of her hand.

He then tucked her arm through his and led her toward the room he'd just left. "I thought you might enjoy a dinner on the terrace. It is quite pleasant outdoors this evening."

Sarah, nervous about once again encountering Mrs. Sorley, said, "Whatever you wish, sir."

He stopped and gave her a kiss which seemed to sap her strength. She melted into him, thinking three Sundays a long time to have to wait while the banns would be read.

He put his finger under her chin, tilting it upward. "That is what I wished for, my dear, but I see you need your nourishment. Come along."

He led her through a small parlor out onto a large flagstone terrace where a table was set for two near a wall that overlooked a small fountain and knot garden. "But what about your sister?"

Sir Evan's eyes took on a dark glint. "My sister has chosen to return to her own home. She left just before five."

"It was because of me, was it not?" Sarah looked up into his face. She didn't want him to ever regret his decision.

He traced a finger along her jaw. "Actually, it was not. She thought she might be able to *tolerate* you. It was the boys that got her ire up."

"The boys! But they are the best-behaved children I have ever known."

"You know that, as do I, but I fear she thought they were like her grandchildren. Even she cannot endure those little demons above a few days." He grinned.

"Then you are not angry." She looked up at him through her lashes.

He shook his head. "I told you, Miss Whiting, that I should take you with thrice as many lads and I meant it. Aggie needed to go home long ago."

Sarah boldly threw her arms around his neck and kissed him. When they drew apart, she said, "Well, if you meant it, I have two young ladies I should like to invite to stay."

Sir Evan's arms tightened around Sarah. "You may fill every bedroom in the house with your friends, my friends, or any other children you rescue, my love—after the honeymoon trip."

"Thank you, dearest one," Sarah whispered as she surrendered to the gentleman's kiss, thoughts of her friends slipping from her mind for the moment, since she was certain they would be welcome at any time.

ABOUT THE AUTHOR

Lynn Collum lives with her family in Alabama. She is currently working on the second installment of her fairy tale regency trilogy, A KISS AT MIDNIGHT (Rose's story), which will be published by Zebra Books in November 2002. Readers can write her at: P.O. Box 814, Valley, AL 36854.